# The Snake That Bowed

# The Snake That Bowed

Edward Seidensticker

after Okamoto Kido

Printed Matter Press

THE SNAKE THAT BOWED
Copyright © 2006 by Edward Seidensticker
All rights reserved.

No part of this book may be reproduced in any form without permission from the publisher, except for brief passages quoted in a review.

Layout & design by Studio Z
Cover design by Joe Zanghi

Published by PRINTED MATTER PRESS
    Yagi Bldg. 4F 2-10-13 Shitaya, Taito-ku,
    Tokyo 110-0004 Japan
    info@printedmatterpress.com
    www.printedmatterpress.com

Printed in Japan

First edition, 2006

ISBN 1-933606-03-7

# Preface

Presented here are three stories from *A Record of Hanshichi's Arrests* (*Hanshichi Torimonocho*), a series of sixty-eight stories published between 1917 and 1936 by Okamoto Kido (1872-1939). Kido was known chiefly as a writer for the Kabuki theater. Hanshichi is a fictional *okappiki*, a police officer under the Tokugawa shogunate. The literal meaning of *okappiki*, a combination of "hill" and "lead" or "take in," strongly suggests snooping and interfering, which were at the heart of Hanshichi's trade. Kido is the given name. It is common practice to use given names for eminent writers of some antiquity. Hanshichi does not seem to have a family name. It was standard for the pre-modem plebeian classes not to.

As a Kabuki writer, Kido was a modernizer. This can mean a number of things, but in his case it seems to mean chiefly combining the realistic characterization of the Western theater with the visual beauty of Kabuki. Probably his most famous play is *Shuzenji Monogatari* (*A Tale of Shuzenji*). Shuzenji is the setting, a spa on the Izu Peninsula southwest of Tokyo. The play centers upon a venerable and distinguished occupation, the carving of masks for the Noh Theater.

Hanshichi was born in 1823 in Nihombashi, the wealthiest part of merchant Edo, pre-modem Tokyo. A few of the stories are hearsay in which Hanshichi does not figure. Through the ones in which he does figure, for about a quarter of a century down to 1867, he is living in Kanda, a less affluent mercantile and artisan district somewhat farther north.

The opening story, that of the severed alien head, is set in 1861. In a very few years the shogunate will be overthrown and Edo will become Tokyo. The other two stories are set some years earlier. I have put them all in the same year so that I can have Hanshichi working on them simultaneously. I do not see that the time shift results in distortion.

In a story written at about the time of the severed-head one, the latest of the three used here, Kido remarks: "If there is any distinguishing feature of these stories, it has to be that glimpses of Edo are caught behind the detective work."

So it is too with these adaptations. I have chosen the stories because I think them interesting and because they are set in very different parts of the Edo complex, and therefore provide a sort of guide to the city. The story of the severed head is largely set in the newly founded port of Yokohama. The morning-glory case is set in aristocratic regions within the outer defenses of Edo Castle. The setting for the case of the snake and the dance teacher is Hanshichi's own plebeian district of merchants and craftsmen.

# I

Hanshichi would have himself a walk down to Yokohama.

He did not seriously consider a means of locomotion other than his feet. Sons of Edo were good walkers. So were daughters, but they had few occasions for going any distance from home, and they were hampered by skirts that bound their ankles together. They had to walk in tiny steps, which were tiring.

Hanshichi's own walking was for the most part limited to a couple of miles north and east of the castle. Though it was not clearly defined, these were essentially the limits of his beat. He was not as much at home in the other directions, and especially the south. A few steps south of home and he was on the castle grounds. There was no law against his venturing into the outer castle precincts, but he did not find them friendly. Even on longer journeys, the son of Edo preferred to walk. When he went to the big cities of western Japan, Kyoto, and Osaka, he generally did so on foot. It was better that way.

Hanshichi did not have many conveyances to chose from. He could have hired a horse or a sedan chair for himself, but he meant to have at least one companion. The two of them would have looked silly mounted in tandem on a horse or knee-to-knee in a sedan chair. There was the expense to consider. He had made inquiry and learned that he and his companion, without horses of their own, would have to hire not two horses but several relays of them. This seemed ridiculous, since the journey from Edo to Yokohama and back would have been nothing for a healthy horse. The reason seemed to be that the people over in the castle, in the greatness of their wisdom, had granted someone a monopoly. The someone was making the most of it. Hanshichi did not object in principle. It was the Edo way, and it was better to have people at useless work than without work. He did not resent many of things the people in the castle did. It was they who brought power to a city which consumed more than it produced.

But he would rather walk.

The rickshaw had not yet been invented. The steam locomotive had been invented, but it had not yet come to Japan. Hanshichi had paid a single visit to Yokohama, and, like most sons of Edo, he had seen many woodcut prints of the town and the great world upon which it opened. He had seen horse-drawn carriages with his own eyes and they were everywhere in the prints. A carriage with horses must give a person feelings of great power. The nearest device Japan had had to that sort of thing was a cart with lumbering oxen.

In any event, walking was more fun. When out upon the town, even the limited part of it that he considered his beat, Hanshichi liked to be among people. His business depended upon knowing everyone everywhere. Even the distance from the top of a horse took him away from people. He would have lost face if he had been seen in a sedan chair. This, except in the high aristocracy, was a womanish thing. People would have laughed.

Yokohama was a very new city. It was one of the treaty ports, opened in obedience to treaties with the Western barbarians, and it had welcomed them, if that was not a misleading word for something forced upon a reluctant nation, only two or three years before. Although it was no more than fifteen miles south of his part of Edo, Hanshichi had had only that one visit. He did not like the idea of Yokohama and the changes it was certain to bring. Yet he was glad for an excuse to go there. The prints assured him that it would be full of curious things. The son of Edo was much given to looking at curious things.

Hanshichi had not made the journey along the Eastern Road to the big cities of western Japan. The occasion had not arisen, and the notion of travel for pleasure was not a part of his world. He had two or three times ventured into the northern provinces on business. He was not alone among sons of Edo in thinking that the city had all the things a person wanted and needed. He was glad the occasion had arisen for an excursion to Yokohama which he could call a business trip. There should be cherry blossoms along the way, and the walk to Yokohama would occupy a day nicely. He lived in Kanda, a plebeian district just north of Edo Castle. The year was 1862. Edo, seat of the shogun, would in not many years become Tokyo.

He expected to enjoy himself. He was an *okappiki*, which could without great distortion be rendered "spy." The literal sense of the word suggested someone who surveyed a scene from an eminence. A decade or so later he might have been given some such title as police detective, but he would have become part of a very different system.

Police agents of Edo relied heavily on hunch and intimidation and often had little by way of material evidence to go on. Many of them were amateurs Hanshichi received a stipend, but the young men who worked for him got only sporadic handouts from Hanshichi himself and gifts from persons who had benefited from their services. The latter in particular could come to considerable sums, because gratitude was for relief from charges of wrongdoing, punishment for which tended to be permanent. Miscreants usually ended up dead or in exile.

Young beginners at police work usually had other jobs. Hanshichi had been more of a professional than most of them. He was born a quarter of the way through the Nineteenth Century in Nihombashi, the heart of mercantile Edo, where his father worked for a dealer in cotton. The father died young, and Hanshichi was taken in by an *okappiki* whose daughter he married and whose policing business he took over. So it would be, presently, with one of the young men who worked for him, though there was a complication along the way. Hanshichi was childless, and would have to adopt a daughter to marry some young police person and perpetuate the family line. It was not a large complication. Such arrangements were common in Edo. For the present, Hanshichi's young men were the next thing to amateurs. Asked why they donated their services for next to nothing, they gave a plausible answer: it was from a sense of duty. Actually they enjoyed the work.

Snooping was in the air of Edo, and interesting. They who were good at it could, without unbridled optimism, look forward to becoming professionals.

They lived in troubled times. The barbarians had appeared in Edo Bay a decade or so before, and a few ports, including Yokohama, had been forced open. Townsmen like Hanshichi did what they could to protect themselves and left the problem of the barbarians to the military elite. This last was divided between supporters of the shogunate, who saw that the barbarians would not go away and would have to be accommodated, and those who held that the Japanese spirit. screwed up to its last measure of resolve, must drive the barbarians into the ocean.

Rumor after rumor passed through Edo that invasion was imminent. The division was essentially between the shogunate, which prevailed in the minds and hearts of Edo itself, and the monarchy, strong especially in the royal capital, Kyoto, and the western and southern provinces. The antibarbarian faction was thus in large measure the royalist faction. This gave anti-barbarians, real and feigned, great license, because everyone paid at least lip service to the monarchy.

The occasion for Hanshichi's stroll down to Yokohama was the case of the severed alien head.

This was brought to his attention by his sister Kume, a music teacher who lived some ten minutes' walk farther from the castle.

After asking his support, which he gave without enthusiasm, for her annual cherry-blossom excursion, an event which she had to arrange and finance if she was to keep her pupils; she asked if he had heard of the case.

She was very pleased that he had not.

"It's always darkest under the lamp," she said.

This was like saying that the king was not the one to ask about goings-on under the palace walls. Hanshichi himself was the lamp, or the king. The severed head had made its appearance very near where he lived and even nearer where Kume herself lived. As she told her story, however, it became clear that lamp-like eminence was not the only reason for his not having heard of the case.

"You know the pawnbroker just down the street?"

"From you or from me?" This was unnecessary. Edo contained a pawnshop in practically every block, and he knew both the one in her block and the one in his perfectly well.

Though she knew that he knew, Kume answered equably that she was referring to the one in her block.

"Last night someone came pounding on the door after closing hours. Mr. Marui was in bed with a cold. The manager went to the door and said through the slit, whoever it was should come back in the morning. The man—after hours it's always a man, usually a drunk on his way to the Yoshiwara or from it—the man said the place would open up if it knew what was good for it. Well, you know how it is these days. Anything can happen to anybody, and the worst things happen to pawnbrokers."

The Yoshiwara was the largest and most famous of the Edo pleasure quarters.

To Hanshichi's analytic mind this was not ideally consistent, but he did not interrupt. The story promised to be interesting.

"So Kizaemon did open up. He wasn't much surprised to see who was there. You know how it is these days. A masked man. He was carrying something tied up in cloth."

Kizaemon, the manager, assumed that it was something for pawning, but it was the severed head. The man was wearing a scarf over his own head. His hair was hidden, and with it his haircut, which would have helped Kizaemon to establish his rank and status.

He belonged, he said, to an armed faction dedicated to ridding the land of barbarians, by force if persuasion did not work. The object he had brought with him should establish their seriousness of purpose. Being composed of masterless samurai, the faction needed money. A loan would be appreciated. He carried the two swords that were the mark of the samurai, but they did not mean much, "these days." If his and his faction's mission was the stated one, then he would indeed be a samurai. Commoners kept out of such matters. A trouble was, however, that extortionists, these days, roved the streets pretending to be anti-barbarian samurai. One of the things people were fond of saying was that measles and masterless samurai were what Edo could most happily do without. Men pretending to be masterless samurai were worse.

Pawnbrokers knew that there was only one way to deal with extortionists. Kizaemon said, calmly and politely, the man should come back in the morning, when either Mr. Marui or the humble assistant now before him would be happy to hear what he had to say. Extortionists were bolder in darkness than in full daylight. There was a cluster of shop boys behind Kizaemon. They could easily have overwhelmed the intruder. But commoners who laid hands on a samurai, even a masterless one, must be prepared to go the ultimate distance. They could easily end up dead or in exile.

"You think I'm not being straight with you."

Kizaemon politely denied any such thought. Lying for the sake of politeness, as well as for the sake of the firm, was not lying at all. Besides, if the man really was a samurai battling for the anti-barbarian royalist cause, civility was more important than at most times. It was always important for pawnbrokers, whose business was not the most popular in the world, and who, as Kume had suggested, were considered fair game.

The man started to untie his bundle. From it came a roundish object wrapped in oil paper on which were nasty reddish smudges. From this he took a severed head. The hair and beard were red. It certainly did have the look of an alien head.

"Where did you get it?"

"Found it on a fellow's shoulders. Don't you want to know why I'm showing it to you? That's much more important."

"I can guess."

The unlovely object established the man's credentials. Who now could doubt that he was a dedicated battler for His Majesty and against the barbarians?

"So?"

"How much do you want?"

The figure named may not have been a king's ransom, exactly, but it was enough to keep a bureaucrat going for several months.

"I can't hand out that kind of money without Mr. Marui's permission."

"Get it."

"He's not well and it's late at night. Maybe a quarter that much will see you through? Strictly as a loan."

They both laughed, though neither of them seemed greatly amused. The man's laugh was sneering. Kizaemon took it to mean that his offer was acceptable. So, money and head in hand, the man departed. He offered to leave the head, but Kizaemon declined. Hanshichi would much rather he had accepted.

"And before he left," said Hanshichi when Kume had finished her story, "he said he would come back and kill everyone in the place if anyone said anything to anyone about what had happened."

"Well, as a matter of fact, yes."

"So everyone but you is a lamp that can't see what's going on underneath it. Why are you the big exception?"

Kume had to think about this for a minute. "I'm your sister," she said, presently seeing the point. "I have a nose for these things."

"Very good. Now, tell me the truth. Remember I'm an officer of the law."

What he said was, more literally, that he was on the shogun's business. "Law" was not a word much used or very well understood in those days.

The truth was that young men from the neighborhood liked to come into her parlor for a cup of tea. Most of her pupils were young women, and many of them were pretty. Among the young men was one from the pawnshop. He had accepted an invitation to join her cherry-blossom outing, and then said, with huge regret, he could not make it. He obviously wanted to get away without explaining, but Kume was not one to let him. She was her brother's sister in having a good nose for the truth. The young man knew it, and did not want to forego the cups of tea. He told her what had happened the night before. She must not tell anyone. Of course she would not. On the grounds that Hanshichi was not just plain anyone, she hurried off to Kanda.

"You're not to forget now. The twenty-first. Bring five or six of the boys with you. Oh, yes, and Sen."

The boys were the amateur investigators who got an occasional tip and had other jobs. Sen was Hanshichi's wife.

"Don't rush off. Tell me about the head. No respectable pawnbroker would hand out that much money without having a good look at the collateral."

"That's a funny word for it. I'd imagine he didn't because it wasn't. Ask him, but don't tell him who told you."

"He'll probably guess. He knows who I am, and you're the closest thing to a bond between us."

"Guessing isn't knowing. He won't know unless you tell him." And she was on her way.

So Hanshichi went off to the pawnshop. The owner was in bed, or occupying quilt and mattress on a floor somewhere. He had indeed been indisposed the night before. The manager received him, and confirmed Kume's story. He did not ask where Hanshichi had heard it. He was a man of experience, and he knew that Hanshichi would plead official privilege if asked. Official privilege was not something which a person of low rank challenged. Merchants ranked lowest in Edo society, and pawnbrokers, unless they were very rich ones, were at the lower fringes of the merchant class.

Was there anything unusual about the man, asked Hanshichi. The mask of course made it impossible to see the face, but the bearing and voice suggested youth. There was nothing peculiar about the speech, which seemed pure Edo.

"Can you describe the head?"

"Not in any detail. It was pretty repulsive. I stayed as far away from it as I could."

"A sense of duty might have overcome your squeamishiness."

"A sense of duty? Did I ask your help?" He would not have spoken so sharply had Hanshichi not also been of the merchant class. "What point would there have been in asking? I did not and do not expect to get the money back."

"But you say that the man took the head out of the wrapping, I believe. Can you describe what you saw?"

"We agreed about one thing. Whatever he said about leaving it with me, he didn't want me to have close look at it. And I didn't want to. Mostly what I saw was red hair. It hung down over the face."

"You think it was a human head?"

"I certainly did last night. It had a strong smell, and not the smell of death. The smell was to cover the smell of death. Fellow wouldn't want to wander around the city trailing that."

"What sort of smell was it?"

"It made me think of a barber shop."

This would be a sickly sweet smell. Traditional hairdos reeked of a sickening oil.

"That could have come from the man that had a head and not the head that had no body."

"Except I sort of think he had a close haircut. There couldn't have been much but skull under the scarf."

At this point Hanshichi decided that a walk to Yokohama was called for. There were not many close-cropped heads in Edo. There were more in Yokohama.

"Not much chance he was one of them." Hanshichi nodded in the direction of the castle. "You should have mobbed him and taken him captive."

"And the head too? Besides, I didn't know how many he had with him."

When Hanshichi got back to Kanda one of his assistants, a young man named Matsu, was awaiting him. He told of an incident east of the river. It was strikingly similar to the incident which Kume had described. Again a pawnbroker was the victim, and again a severed head was used to negotiate a loan. The distance between the two pawnshops was easily walkable.

"I found this just inside the door," said Matsu, taking a wallet from his kimono and a not immediately identifiable object from the wallet.

He handed it to Hanshichi.

It was a hair.

"Looks sort of foreign to me. How does it look to you."

"Good work, for a young fellow."

Matsu smiled happily. "They'd scrubbed the floor but they missed it."

It was a rufous hair. Hanshichi could imagine it in an alien beard or on an alien head. It could have been dyed, but it was not from a Japanese head. Oriental hair was several times coarser than Occidental hair. Hanshichi had picked this piece of information up in the course of the talk that went around about foreigners. Coarse hair may not have been one of the more striking features of beauty, but Hanshichi was rather proud of having it. He could not think of a beast that would have such hair. It was long, and Japanese cats and dogs had short hair. He would have to consult an expert.

"Good," said Hanshichi again. "Where did you hear about it?"

"Through the grapevine." He doubtless meant his fellows in the somewhat amateur police force. He actually used the expression "potato runner." Japan did not have many grapes in those days.

"Did the pawnbroker get a close look at the head."

"He only got close enough to see that it had red hair and was pretty disgusting, all smeared over with blood."

Hanshichi had little doubt that the culprits were the same, or that they had walked.

"It was a real head?"

"He wouldn't have been so anxious to get it out of the place if it hadn't been. Or if he hadn't thought it was."

"How would you like a trip down to Yokohama?"

"By myself?"

"Would you be afraid to go by yourself?"

"Of course not. But it's always good to have company."

Sons of Edo were a gregarious lot.

"I mean to go too."

"It should be fun."

He meant it. He was young, and he had not been to Yokohama. They agreed to set out after breakfast the following morning.

In the afternoon Hanshichi visited the constable's office by the river and then his expert. The constable's office had heard of no decapitated barbarians. Hanshichi had been sure that this would be the case, and had decided on the trip to Yokohama even before he made sure of it. The murder of a barbarian would be an event so remarkable that one need not be a police agent to hear of it. There were almost none in Edo, and everyone knew that public policy was to leave the few alone.

The citizenry of Edo was not strongly inclined to go against public policy. America and five European countries had legations or agencies in Edo, all of them in the southern part of the city, the part nearest the relative security of Yokohama, and most of them in temples. Their combined staff had never come to more than perhaps two dozen men. Fewer now resided in Edo than a year or two before. Most of them (the Americans were the exception) had withdrawn to Yokohama, for there had been ugly incidents. If the commoner was uniformly polite to them, such was not always the case with the samurai. The ugliest of the incidents was the murder of a Dutch interpreter on the staff of the American legation.

So Hanshichi had concluded even before his visit to the magistracy that if he was to inquire into the incident of the severed head, and his dignity would suffer if he did not, Yokohama was the place to start inquiring.

He took the hair to a Holland doctor, as they were called, a practitioner of Western medicine. These too were few in number, but the number was rapidly rising. The doctor offered no surprises. He confirmed what Hanshichi had thought, that the hair was too fine to have come from an Oriental head. Nor did he think, and here Hanshichi had been in doubt, that it came from an animal. It was not, certainly, from a Japanese animal, and controls over barbarian animals were strict. The likelihood was strong that it was from the head of an alien human.

So, concluded Hanshichi, this was as far as the resources of Edo could bring him.

Two others among Hanshichi's disciples, if that was the word for them, were inclined to accompany them as far as Shinagawa. They had no good reason except that the day was fine and the more company the merrier. No one could object, if they had nothing else to do. A walk of ten miles, about the distance to Shinagawa and back, was nothing for a son of Edo. Hanshichi suspected another reason, but did not remark upon it. Shinagawa was the first wayside station on the road to Kyoto, and wayside stations—all of them—were provided with drink and pretty, compliant waitresses, called geisha by some. The stations were too close together to be, for even a mediocre walker, a day's walk one to the next. People dawdled. Hanshichi and Matsu expected to use less than a day for the walk to the third station, Kanagawa. Hanshichi suspected that the others would dawdle at Shinagawa.

It was a beautiful day. As they set out Hanshichi thought, as he had thought many times before, what a fine place Kanda was to live in. There he was among his own people, small merchants and workmen. Mikawa, his particular part of Kanda, was neither too rich nor too poor. Its workmen were well known, for a most particular kind of skill. They were experts at keeping banners under control. Many processions, and in particular funeral processions, required banners, and these could be rebellious on a windy day. People from all over town came to Mikawa when they needed banner men.

Richer and sterner places were near at hand. Nihonbashi, Japan Bridge, the heart of mercantile Edo, was a few minutes' walk away, down a pleasant canal. Nihombashi was point zero. From it distances to the rest of the country were measured. Roads to the east were said to go down, roads to the west went up. Maps of Edo were conventionally oriented westwards. This was because Kyoto was the royal capital. Nihombashi was richer than Kyoto, however.

Even closer were the outer grounds of the castle. Hanshichi enjoyed an occasional walk to Nihombashi, where the great merchants, Mitsui and the like, held forth. He had been born in Nihombashi, but to a family that would not have been too rich for Kanda. He did not enjoy going across a moat to castle grounds, but sometimes business took him there. In addition to being neither too rich nor too poor, Kanda was central.

The morning was still young when they passed Nihombashi. It was mercantile Edo at its grandest. The grandeur was most evident in dry-goods stores. In the largest of these the Mitsui name was its most conspicuous. A person visiting Edo for the first time, Hanshichi sometimes thought, might conclude that all it cared about was food and clothes. And, he would add mentally, the person would not be far from right. The visitor would have to stay around a while and do some exploring to learn that sex was also of some importance. The officials tried, sometimes more energetically than at other times, to keep it out of sight. They were at the moment having a seizure of energy. But, he would add further, the readily apparent predilections of the city were those of all the Japanese cities he had visited. They who had been to the great cities of the west, Kyoto and Osaka, had not been filled with admiration. Tinhorn Edo, was the general view.

As they walked south along the Eastern Highway, they were in less affluent districts, and ever more so. A sense grew that they were nearing the *basue*, "the end of the place." Ginza too had big dry-goods establishments and plenty of restaurants, but elegant fabrics were less common, in the shops along the way, than footwear, showers of which hung from cords in shop fronts. Ginza had always been a working-class district. It took its name, "Silver Seat," from the shogun's mint, in the northern part of the district. The mint had moved elsewhere, and Ginza had grown decrepit. Like Kanda, it was a place of workmen and small merchants, but they clearly did not do as well there as in Kanda.

"A drink for your thoughts, young fellows. But not till we get to Shinagawa. I mean no drinks, not no thoughts."

"*Basue*," said Matsu.

In a privileged position, for only he would accompany the master all the way to Yokohama, he could speak for the rest. They seemed to agree.

"Yes, now it is," said Hanshichi. "But the end will be the beginning, and when we get to Shimbashi you'll see why. My advice to you is to invest your money in Ginza."

Shimbashi, "New Bridge," was the one they would cross next.

"Ha ha," said Matsu. And he added: "Why?"

"Wait for the bridge. Meanwhile we have these geisha. What do they tell you?"

Matsu giggled.

"What they should tell you is that you're right. We're at the end of the place. That's where they keep geisha. As I'm sure you know better than I do."

Off to their right, clearly visible on the back street next in from the main Eastern Highway, was a cluster of houses more elegant than the general Ginza run. From them emerged sounds of music lessons. Though the rule was not infallible, geisha did commonly proclaim that a place was at its end. That is where the authorities tried to keep ladies of the night.

Hanshichi and his companions crossed Shimbashi, a narrow and shabby bridge compared to Nihombashi.

"See?"

"Some of us might not see, exactly," said Matsu.

"Ginza has the end-of-the-place look. Spread out before you now is the outside-the- place look."

"I see what you mean," said Matsu.

Ginza may not have looked very prosperous but it did look urban. Beyond Shimbashi the city scattered. The most conspicuous complex of manmade objects in the view from Shimbashi was a cemetery. It was a very special sort of cemetery, to be sure, one of two in which lay shoguns and their near relatives; but Edo was not friendly to cemeteries. They lay on its outskirts. That the presence of death was a defilement was given as the reason for the unfriendliness. Hanshichi suspected that greed was a better explanation. The rich and powerful wanted large tracts of land near the center of things, which was to say, the castle.

More to the point was the fact that there was unoccupied land before them. Nothing of the sort was to be observed in Ginza. As usual, Hanshichi was right. The center of Edo was compact (except for tracts occupied by the rich and powerful) and they had left it behind.

"So put your money in Ginza."

They awaited explanation.

When none was forthcoming one of them said: "Why? Land must be cheaper out here in the sticks."

"I've seen you wasting time over the penny prints that come up from Yokohama."

"No, not wasting time. The future is in them. They show you all the things we will have tomorrow or the day after. For instance: the big iron coaches that roar along on tracks pouring out smoke. We'll have them in no time. There's already talk of them over there." Hanshichi gestured in the direction the castle would have been in if they had been at home. Instead he got the cemetery, which would do as well.

"So?" said Matsu, when it became clear that Hanshichi meant to say no more.

"So where will the coaches and their rails go to? Not through the Ginza clutter to Nihombashi, where any sensible rails would go. That would be too much trouble and expense. They'll go to Shimbashi. So Ginza at the end of the place will be Ginza at the beginning of the place. Put money into it and you'll be rich in a few years."

"Someone could just touch a match to Ginza. That would take care of it. With the right wind it would be gone in a couple of hours."

"The words of a true son of Edo," said Hanshichi.

"Or someone to lead us into the new age," said one of the others.

They all had a good laugh.

"Why don't you put money into it?" asked Matsu.

"I don't have any."

They all laughed some more. It was an even merrier outing than they would have expected.

## 2

From time to time cherry petals drifted through the mild air. They could look forward to fine stands of cherry here and there in the southern part of the city, though in this regard Hanshichi thought that his northern part had the better of it. If they had wished to take the time they could have gone into the cemetery. There they could have paid homage to convention and mused upon the uncertainty of life and the melancholy beauty of blossoms in their prime.

The cemetery lay a short distance to their right as they proceeded southwards. Its elevations were wonderfully fresh and vernal.

"I wonder," said Hanshichi, "whether your noggins have room for one more profound thought." He looked at them. They looked uniformly eager. "Those penny prints from Yokohama. I"m sure you've noticed the gaudy colors they over there," and he gestured broadly in the direction of the bay and the ocean beyond, "paint their houses. Why do you suppose we don't paint ours at all? Why do we leave them to get browner and browner and grayer and grayer?"

"Maybe because we like it that way," said Matsu, who had become the designated spokesman for the younger element.

"Not a bad answer, even if it does raise all sorts of new questions. But there's a better reason. A more Japanese reason. The two mean about the same thing. You'll see down there."

He pointed ahead, to a spot at which the road seemed to turn right.

Though no one told them to, they walked a little faster.

At the curve the road emerged upon the bay. They paused to admire the view. Hanshichi did not elaborate on his earlier pronouncement.

"So?" said Matsu finally.

"So what?"

Feeling rebuffed, Matsu inquired no further. He did his best to look curious, however. It seemed to work.

"See how much brighter it looks after all that brown and gray. Which is a very good reason for having brown and gray."

Though not at all sure that this was true, Matsu nodded. He feared that a lecture was coming. The other two were silent. They may have feared the same thing.

The lecture began, about how their ancestors got things right. Matsu was glad that Shinagawa was near. They could have their drink, and maybe find other things to talk about. Or maybe silence would be permitted. Matsu did not disagree about the superiority of their ancestors, but he had heard it all before.

Shinagawa was a pleasant place. Its shops and inns and drinking places hugged the bay shore. Choosing one of these last, they settled down on clean straw matting for their drinks. It was too early for lunch, but a person did not drink sake without tidbits. So they had tidbits with cold sake, best for a warm spring day. The way they had come followed the bay. So, for a time, did the way they were to go. White sails moved back and forth across the bay. Some of the boats were for cargo, most for fishing. Sons of Edo, and daughters as well, held that the finest fish in the land and (of course) in the world came from Edo Bay. Along the strand, nets hung from poles to dry. They were like a distant view of jagged mountains.

On the eminence above them was the most famous stand of cherries in the southern part of the city. Shinagawa was held by tradition to be the southern extreme, though there was an element of fiction in this view. Considerable tracts of open land lay between it and the tombs of the shoguns, where the city might more properly have been held to begin. The eminence was called Mansion Hill. There must once have been an impressive building atop it, probably associated with some regime or other. Hanshichi could not have identified either building or regime. Neither could the younger generation. The stand of cherries had until recently been a favorite place for springtime revelry.

They could only view it from afar, because the precincts were blocked off. The British legation, the most aggressive of them, had demanded a building of its own, and was getting one, right there where much of the south side of Edo had always gone to view blossoms.

"Wonder if they'll ever finish it," said Matsu.

"Of course not," said Hanshichi. "They don't want to. That's why they picked the worst possible place for it."

Even in his own northern regions, and even among commoners, he had heard grumblings that the famous blossoms were being turned over to unfeeling barbarians. They must be much louder in the southern regions they had just come through, and he had heard reports from on high that they were loud indeed among the samurai. Someone would burn the unfinished structure down, and the shogunate would say that it had done its best, and not even the British could disagree.

Hanshichi and Matsu presently set off from Shinagawa. It did not surprise them that the others seemed in no great hurry to get back to Kanda.

For several miles beyond Shinagawa, the Kyoto highway followed the coast. Then it did not so much turn away from the coast as have the coast turn away from it The alluvial lands along the lower reaches of the only large river they would cross pushed out into the bay. The coast made Hanshichi a little nervous. Edo was not really a maritime city, and the great threat to the land and to Edo hegemony had come across water from the east.

It was the most important highway in the land, and it was little more than a footpath. It was crowned with pines, however, which lent distinction. Lord Tokugawa had lined the road to his family tombs in the north country with towering cedars, and might have said, though no one thought to ask him, that it was the grandest road in the land. Pines were more diminutive, but cedars came in only one shape, and pines came in many. Crowned with pines, it seemed a rather grand highway.

They were ferried across the river.

"We could have a try at wading or swimming," said Hanshichi.

"And look like waders or swimmers when we get to Yokohama?"

They took the ferry. It was the only part of the journey that they did not execute on their own four feet.

They did not dally at the second station, comfortably inland. They wondered whether the other two were still dallying at Shinagawa. Shortly before they reached the third station, Kanagawa, the road came out on the bay once more. There was a vernal laziness in the lapping of wavelets on the shore. White sails, mostly fishing and shell-taking boats, though there could have been cargo boats to and from Nagoya and Osaka among them, moved lazily across the waters.

"A fellow could stand a nap," said Matsu.

"I'll buy you a drink," said Hanshichi, "but you won't get a nap."

They stopped at a little bayside stall for their drink.

As they sat with their sake, they had the future on one side of them and the past on the other. The road and the station, with their pine trees and their low wooden buildings, had changed little in a century and more. Traffic was leisurely and seemed generally light-hearted, though an occasional samurai on horseback glowered at the world as he passed.

A traveler in a guarded sedan chair would be of the upper orders, and if the blinds were down probably a woman and not of the highest orders, for women of the nobility were allowed to travel only a short distance south of Edo. This was to assure that their lords and masters were up to no mischief in the remote provinces, although it was general knowledge in Edo that serious mischief was in progress. It was the chief source of unrest in the city.

And over across an inlet lay the future in the form of Yokohama, an object, for Edo townsmen like Hanshichi and Matsu, of intense interest and unease. Under the first foreign treaty, with the Americans, Kanagawa itself was to have been opened for trade; but Kanagawa lay on the busy road to Kyoto and Osaka. It would be next to impossible to keep alien and domestic persons separated from one another. The shogunate quickly saw that Yokohama, a fishing village across the inlet which was to become its harbor, would in this crucial respect be preferable.

They industriously set about making it resemble Deshima, the island in Nagasaki Bay where the Dutch had done business and kept to themselves through the centuries of the Tokugawa shogunate. Nature had put water on three sides of Yokohama and now a ditch was dug along the fourth side, making it, like Deshima, an island. The authorities hoped that the outsiders would get the message.

The Americans had been at the start of it, but these days the British were dominant, not to say domineering. There was disagreement between British businessmen and diplomats. The latter were intent upon keeping the shogunate to the letter of the treaties (several followed the American one). The former saw that Yokohama, with deep water immediately in front of it, would be better for trade. The legations went on pretending that Kanagawa had opened, but presently had to recognize that in fact Yokohama had. At the rate Yokohama was growing it would soon engulf Kanagawa in any event.

The shogunate did not encourage its subjects to keep more company with the aliens than was absolutely necessary. The security of these last was also on the bureaucratic mind. Aware of how few defenses it had against them, it did not want ugly incidents (although Hanshichi may have been right in thinking that it invited at least one by choosing a popular blossom-viewing place for the site of the new British legation). A popular word for the trading port was Kannai, "inside the barriers," with reference to several guard posts along the waters by which it was surrounded. Their function was to turn back threats and discourage streams of traffic in either direction.

The system was not a complete success. Overnight outings to Yokohama were popular among Edo townsmen, and foreigners liked to gallop their horses up and down the Edo-Kyoto road. From this diversion too were certain to arise ugly incidents. *Daimyo* processions passed up and down the road. Their escorts had a uniform response to any suggestion of discourtesy: off with his head.

Having finished their sake and accompaniments, Hanshichi and Matsu took a ferry across the inlet. On the far shore they went first to the magistrate's office, in the hills above the port. The imagined ropes that marked off areas of jurisdiction among Edo police agents were not always as clear as they might have been. Agents were always venturing into gray zones. Since they were all drinking companions, there was seldom serious trouble. On this occasion, however, Hanshichi was clearly beyond his ropes. A call on the magistrate's office was asked for, to report his business and ask cooperation. While he was about it, Hanshichi meant to inquire after an old friend among Edo police agents who had been posted to Yokohama. This proved unnecessary. There he was when they came out, at the gate to the magistrate's office.

"Everyone knows about it when Hanshichi comes to town," he said. His name was Goro.

"And I suppose you know what we came for."

"You weren't whispering. I have a thing or two to tell you."

The three went to arrange lodgings for the two who had come strolling down from Edo. This they did at the inn at which Hanshichi had stayed on his first visit. Then they went across a bridge and past a guard post for a look at the town. They had no trouble passing it, and probably would have had little even if they had not been on the shogun's business. The Japanese government thought that, with one line of defense in Kanagawa and another at the bridges into Yokohama, it had done everything reasonably possible. Undesirable elements made their way into Yokohama even so.

"We've had some cases just like the one you told them about," said Goro as they walked the short distance to Honchodori, Main Street—a broad avenue leading through the foreign settlement that was the east half and the Japanese town that was the west half of the new international port. The two halves met just inland from the docks and the customs house.

Having entered from the west, they did the Japanese town first. The fronts of the little shops were open to the street, even as in Edo. They were like little stages open to the passing audience, and piled high with stage properties. Hanshichi was struck by the number of curio shops, more by a good deal than on his earlier visit. Such foreigners as were to be observed were mostly Chinese, recognizable not so much by their features as by their grooming. Hanshichi would have said that there was no reason for a Japanese to come all the way to Yokohama in search of curios. In this he seemed to be wrong. Chinese were likely to take a lofty attitude towards curios of Japanese origin, as most of them were.

There were also shops purveying Western wares. Clocks and watches were especially popular. They did not take up much space, and they were so utterly Western. The shops were all new. They could scarcely be anything else. They were in traditional styles, however. They could have been in one of the less flourishing parts of Edo.

The dress of the Japanese men ran a gamut, or most of one. There was pure Japanese, of course, and there was what might have been pure Western had it been worn more comfortably. Shoes seemed to present a particular problem, which only the genuinely committed could make themselves wrestle with. There were all manner of intermediate stages, Japanese on top and Western on the bottom, Western on top and Japanese on the bottom, the two randomly mixed. Hair styles too ran a gamut, and there seemed to be no correlation between the one gamut and the other. Western dress would be appended to a Japanese hairdo, a cropped head, stiff hair shooting off in every direction, would surmount a Japanese ensemble. As was the way with frontier towns, men greatly outnumbered women. Such Japanese women as they saw remained traditional both in dress and in coiffure.

The animals interested him as much as the people, both the animals alive and scampering about and those stiff and cold. He would not have imagined that such a variety of dogs was possible. Native dogs were all of them very much the same size and shape. Here were dogs of all shapes, in sizes ranging from that of the rat to that of the elephant. Or so he imagined. He had never seen an elephant, though he had seen many rats. Then there was a butcher shop. An ugly, hairy foreigner was hacking animals to pieces. The shop was in the Japanese town, though the meat had to be for the tables of foreigners, most of it, at any rate. Japanese had only just begun consuming beef. The explanation had to be that foreigners did not like living near the place, and required Japanese to do it.

"But we'll get rid of them all some day," said Hanshichi.

His companions may or may not have heard. Neither answered.

When they could see the customs house, taller than anything in the Japanese town, they turned to have a look at the harbor. It was full of masts. He saw no vessels that he would have identified as Japanese except the lighters, which seemed to bear chiefly thread and fabrics. Going out of Japan were silks and coming in were cottons. There were also large quantities of tea, all coming in. Was there enough silk to pay for it all, Hanshichi wondered.

The plaza behind the docks was full of people, as full as Nihombashi, the busiest part of mercantile Edo. Most of the faces were turned out to sea. Hanshichi read yearning on many of them. He did not himself have any great desire to leave Edo for any other place in the world, but he could understand the frustration of those who did. Despite the "opening" of the country, it was difficult to go abroad. A willingness to take risks was required, for the government still did not like the idea of having its people see foreign places. Having a foreign accomplice willing to take similar risks was a help.

They saw a foreign woman, a different shape, even when fully dressed, from Japanese women. She was narrow at the waist and full at the skirt.

"The doctor's wife," said Goro.

"The doctor's wife. That would be—"

"Yes. Mrs. Hebon."

Which would be Mrs. Hepburn, the wife of an American medical missionary who had arrived in Yokohama very shortly after the opening of the port and was already very famous in Edo. He was credited with almost miraculous powers. Everyone with something incurable tried to see him.

"Where does he live?"

"Way down there." Goro pointed towards the hills rising

above the eastern extremity of the foreign settlement. As the settlement expanded, they were to become the Yokohama Bluff, the most desirable address for foreigners and for "buttery" Japanese as well. These were Japanese with foreign taste.

"Maybe I'll introduce myself when we get there. No hurry."

You must have taken leave of your senses, said the expression on Goro's face.

"I suppose someone somewhere might call her beautiful," said Matsu.

"She has a good skin."

"I suppose so. If you like mustaches on women."

"You say you had some cases," said Hanshichi to Goro.

"Good old Hanshichi. Doesn't miss a thing."

"So you've stopped having them and we've started having them. What does that suggest, young fellow?" This last was addressed to Matsu.

"That whoever was doing it here has moved to Edo."

"Which piece of information is enough to make our little walk worth the trouble. Have you had anything to do with these cases?"

"More than anyone, I might say, without seeming to brag."

"And what have you come up with?"

"A problem foreigner or two that we're watching."

"What makes you think it might be a foreigner? Almost anyone could come in past that gate."

"Just a hunch, mostly." It has been noted that hunches were important in the police work of the shogunate. "But a little more than that. A foreigner could murder a foreigner and cut off his head and we would never find out about it. A Japanese couldn't."

They went into a shop that sold foreign things. This seemed more sensible than all the shops selling Japanese things. Some day there might be large numbers of foreign visitors buying Japanese wares, but the day had not yet come. Many of the Japanese wares were for people who did not know very much. Hanshichi thought it would be pleasant and wise to take a foreign object or two back as gifts, for his wife and perhaps his sister. He rescued a blue-eyed doll with an exceedingly sweet face from a clutter of vases and basins and ewers, and while he was about it bought a glass vase too, all purple and red. He thought it a little extreme, but it was unmistakably foreign, and that was what mattered.

They started down the half of main street leading through the foreign settlement. It was by no means as open as the Japanese. Fences and walls predominated. The most imposing of the buildings, just east of the customs house, was (of course) British, and it did not seem interested in the retail customer. There was nothing to suggest that Japanese were forbidden entrance, but there was nothing either suggesting that they were welcome. He did notice a difference, however. The large establishments were more uninviting than the smaller.

They came to the stream that bounded the foreign settlement on the east. Beyond it rose the hills. Yokohama itself was utterly flat.

"There is Dr. Hebon's place," said Goro, pointing down towards the harbor.

"Did you bring that hair with you, young fellow?"

"That hair?"

"The hair you collected in Fukagawa."

Fukagawa was the district east of the river where the later of the two pawnbroker incidents two nights before had occurred.

"No. Should I have? Anyway I gave it to you."

"So you did. And what do you know here it is."

"What hair? Why?" said Goro.

"I'll just see what he thinks about it."

"Not me," they both said.

"You take on the worst Japanese rascals morning noon and night day after day month in and month out and you're afraid of a foreigner who can't be anything but a gentleman even if he might try to convert you? It doesn't make sense, not a particle of sense."

He went in.

The reception room was crowded. It had a board floor and chairs. Some of the waiting patients were seated on chairs, but more preferred the floor. Many of them did indeed look as if only a miracle could save them from the crematory.

It would not have occurred to Hanshichi not to take advantage of his position and put himself at the head of the line. The Japanese at the reception desk said that the doctor would see him when he had finished an amputation (or something—the term was one Hanshichi was not familiar with, though it sounded brutal).

Uncomfortable among such varieties, and so many of them extreme, of malformation and disease, Hanshichi was glad that the wait was not a long one. The doctor, who was surrounded by sinister-looking implements, seemed to be (though a person had trouble guessing the age of foreigners) on the younger side of middle age. Such of his face as showed above a grizzled beard was solemn but not forbiddingly stern.

He asked, a twinkle in his eyes, what he might do for the shogun. His Japanese was good, considering that he could not have been in Japan before the opening of the ports.

Hanshichi took out the hair and told about it. He did not leave any details out for reasons of secrecy, though there were details that did not seem very useful. He of course told whence the hair had come and where the severed head had put in its appearances.

"And you've come all the way to Yokohama to show it to me?"

Apologizing for not having mentioned the Holland doctors of Edo, Hanshichi said he had thought it a good idea to go directly to the source of their wisdom.

The doctor seemed to think this a good one. He laughed merrily.

He examined the hair with a magnifying glass and then with an instrument the likes of which Hanshichi had not seen.

"What did your Holland doctors say about it?"

"That it was not from an Oriental head or a Japanese animal. So it was most probably from a human being or an animal of the Western Seas."

"The former. Very little doubt about it."

"May I venture to ask whether your highness has heard of any troubles that might help to account for it?"

"Oh, I hear of troubles aplenty, but the only murder I can think of just at the moment is that nice Dutchman you people did in. Gifted young fellow. I suppose you people know your business, but it seems a waste."

Hanshichi saw little point in trying to explain that he himself was not of the samurai class, and had as little sympathy with the more flamboyant activities of that class as the doctor seemed to have.

"Tell me about the troubles."

"I would hardly know where to begin, and you may have noticed that there are people waiting to see me. You will forgive me for mentioning this, I am sure."

The doctor would have heard if a foreigner had murdered a foreigner, and Hanshichi felt strongly that the doctor was being honest with him.

"I'll only take a minute more of your time. But just think for a minute if you will of someone who might fit the model taking a fuzzy sort of shape in my mind. It's not a very good mind, but it's always putting models together. I sort of see someone who works with foreigners and needs money, really needs it, right away."

"Well, if you want something that will fit about everything, there's the Thompson case. It involves everything you could look for in this town, including sex. Of sex we have plenty in this town, and you'll understand that I'm not the person best qualified to talk about it." There was the twinkle once more. The doctor was no prude. "It could quite well be the most important factor. And in the Thompson case you have both Japanese and foreigners to pick from."

"What riches," said Hanshichi. He had never thought taking on the doctor such a daunting task, and he was thinking it less and less so. "I hope telling me about the Thompson case will not put you too far behind with your patients."

Since the doctor proceeded to tell him about it in some detail, Hanshichi was able to reassure himself that it would not.

The Thompson case centered upon a young British person named Lloyd. He worked for a trading company named Thompson.

The doctor did not know how good he was at his work, but that he was altogether too good at play seemed clear to everyone. He had given himself up to an obsessive fondness for the new Yokohama pleasure quarter, and especially for a courtesan who worked in the largest and most ornate establishment, Terrapin House.

Hanshichi had had a look at the quarter on his earlier visit. The shogunate had built a new quarter, a short distance inland and not all far from Dr. Hepburn's establishment, ready for the opening of the port. The assumption was that gentlemen of America, China, and Europe, even as gentlemen of Japan, would want and need a pleasure quarter. The terrapin place, Hanshichi had to admit, was grander than anything he knew in Edo. He had heard that it was modeled on something in Nagasaki, which had had long experience of foreigners.

Be that as it may, Lloyd needed money. The head of his firm was convinced that salary and savings were not enough to cover his expenses. He could find no sign that anything was missing from the Thompson till. So where was the money coming from? He consulted the Yokohama magistrate's office, and attention turned to a Japanese connection. A Japanese employee of the company had first taken Lloyd to the quarter and gone with him on subsequent visits. He too was fond of someone there, and Lloyd paid the bills. The Japanese in question seemed to be from the eastern part of Edo. Both the recent pawnbroker incidents might be said to have occurred in the eastern part of the city, the later one more so than the earlier one. It was easy to fire the Japanese, and fired he was. The Englishman was another matter. The legation was sure to insist that he be sent home.

"The British, you know."

Hanshichi was not sure that he did know. But he knew what he needed to know for the moment. He thanked the doctor for his time and all this valuable information, and started to bow himself out.

"We have Bible classes every Sunday morning, if you might be interested."

Hanshichi said he was much honored to be thought worthy,

but it would not be practical for him to come from Edo every Sunday morning. As a matter of fact he was not quite sure when Sunday was.

"I always have a try," said the doctor, smiling. "I wish you success with this interesting case."

"You were saying?" Hanshichi said to Goro, who had not ventured into the waiting room. Neither had Matsu.

"Something, I'm sure."

"Something about how you people thought the culprit must be a foreigner. I think maybe you were going to go on and tell me something about your investigations. That would be nice. But let me tell you something interesting I heard from Dr. Hepburn. Pleasant fellow, Dr. Hepburn. You'll like him if you screw up courage to introduce yourself, and he won't try very hard to convert you. I wonder if you people might have heard about the interesting thing."

And he told of the Thompson case.

"That's one of the ones we're looking into."

"About your pawnbroker, young fellow."

"My pawnbroker? I don't have a regular one."

"The one over east of the river night before last. Did you ask him what the man with the head sounded like?"

"I didn't talk to him at all."

"That was negligent of you."

"But it was over east of the river."

Matsu seemed to have a clearer sense of roped-off zones than Hanshichi himself.

"True. I did ask mine. He said that the man (I assume that it was the same man in both cases) sounded exactly like Edo to him. Would a foreigner sound exactly like Edo?"

"I wouldn't know. I've never talked to one."

"What opportunities you've missed. I've just been talking to one. Pleasant fellow. The best that can be said for his Japanese is that it's understandable if you don't let your attention wander. The man my pawnbroker talked to was not a foreigner. I'm not saying, don't misunderstand me, that no foreigner was involved."

He now addressed Goro. "Tell me more about what you've found out. The Thompson thing. Other things too, if you think I might be interested."

"The man Saburo seems to be from Fukagawa." This was the district east of the river where the later of the incidents had occurred.

"Who's Saburo?" asked Matsu.

"Give your imagination free reign and see if you can't guess. You need practice."

"The Thompson man that went to the whorehouse and got fired."

"Good. Very good." And to Goro: "Continue, please. We're both following you. At the moment, anyhow. Did Saburo go back to Fukagawa when he got fired?"

"We aren't sure where he now rests his head, but he still turns up at Terrapin House most nights."

"With the Englishman?"

"They don't always go in and out together, but they see each other. They don't seem to be on very good terms. But we can't be sure. They always talk something foreign. English, probably. Dutch doesn't get you very far these days."

"Why don't you have some foreigner eavesdrop on them in English?"

"It's a point of pride."

"You've been in this business long enough not to have much of that."

"Results are what matter."

"Well, actually, it's more. Big things are involved. We can't let them think we aren't capable of running things by ourselves."

He was referring to extraterritoriality, a burning issue since the opening of the ports. Foreigners were not subject to Japanese courts. When something concerning one or several of them came up the consuls had jurisdiction. It was among the issues of the day that really troubled Hanshichi. A consular court was for him laxness and corruption, and if Japanese law was good enough for Japanese it should be good enough for foreigners. Sometimes, it was true, he was not entirely sure what Japanese law was, since they who made it were not saying.

"I think we should go have a look at Terrapin House after dinner." "Goody," said Matsu. Or a word to that effect.

"I'll go with you," said Goro "I can point them out."

## 3

After dinner, which they had at their inn, they went to the pleasure quarter. They had to pass a barrier and a bridge once more, for only thus could they reach the quarter, which lay behind the main part of Yokohama, and was isolated by marshes.

Once more they walked eastwards on Main Street, through the Japanese town. When they reached the broad street leading inland from the customs house and dividing Japanese town from foreign, they turned south, and soon were on a causeway through the marshes. These, all along the south side of the town, with only the quarter jutting out into them, gave the isolation which the government thought proper for an international settlement. it was naive, thought Hanshichi, if they thought that marshes and isolation would long survive. The mercantile spirit was already busily destroying them, with reclamation and new building. Like most Edo townsmen, he was not bitterly unhappy with things as they were, and would as soon have let them be; and on the other hand it was good to see the mercantile spirit threatening grave revenge upon them who spurned it. His part of Edo was strongly mercantile.

A few steps after the causeway turned at a right angle they were at the only bridge crossing the moat around the quarter. Like the rest of Edo, Hanshichi knew what happened as a result of such arrangements when the Yoshiwara, the most famous of pleasure quarters, on the northern outskirts of Edo, burned down. This it did from time to time. Women were incinerated by the score and by the hundred. He rather hoped that the women of this new quarter did not prove to be excessively well-endowed. It was less painful to think of the incineration of a homely woman than of a beauty.

"Will we go into one of the houses?" asked Matsu.

"If you want. But you won't have to."

"And have a woman apiece?"

"Are you suggesting that we might share one?" said Hanshichi.

"If you want. Just go in and look around if you want. You'll see. They have guided tours."

"An unguided one would be more fun," said Hanshichi.

Inside the gate was an avenue lined with cherries, now in bloom, and willows, and lighted with a myriad of paper lanterns. The willow was a ubiquitous symbol of the pleasure quarters, "cities of flower and willow," and most quarters, such as the Yoshiwara, had both willows and cherries. The bustle and stir, thought Hanshichi, were not inferior to the Yoshiwara. Though the new Yokohama quarter had been built to answer to the needs of foreigners, only one in a hundred of the persons swarming the street looked to be of European origins. And all of them had made their way past guards and guard posts. The authorities may have seen that the local trade was not enough to keep the quarter going.

Terrapin House, some distance from the gate, was the oldest and most imposing of the houses, many of which were little more than wooden huts. It could have passed for an ornate piece of traditional Japanese architecture, such as a bathhouse or a temple. The chief concession to the presumed sensibilities of foreigners was a generous use of glass. Hanshichi saw that little about it had changed since his earlier visit. The court just inside the entrance was two stories high. On the ground level a bridge of vermilion lacquer led across a pond. In the grandest of rooms, on the second level, was the famous chandelier, wonderfully ornate, glass in every direction. The light was by candle, sometimes enclosed in lanterns and glass chimneys, more often exposed on candlesticks, some of which were also wonderfully ornate. As on his first visit, Hanshichi thought it grander than anything he knew in mercantile Edo. With aristocratic Edo he was less familiar, though he could not remember having seen a glass chandelier in such aristocratic mansions as his duties had required him to visit. He preferred to have nothing to do with aristocrats, but sometimes he could not avoid them.

"How much does it cost?" asked Matsu.

"To have a woman or just to have a look?"

"Never was much for sightseeing."

"This place costs more than any of the others."

"Which is the cheapest?"

"I think we should watch the parade for a while," said Hanshichi. "Maybe you can control yourself, for a while?"

Matsu nodded, without enthusiasm.

It would not do, they soon saw, to join the parade. It would not do for Hanshichi, at any rate. He kept being recognized. He withdrew to the partial concealment of a large weeping-cherry. People also recognized Goro, but in his case it did not matter. His presence in the quarter asked no explanation. Hanshichi's might frighten people off, and he could think of no very good way to know whom it had frightened.

Leaving the others to do as they would with Terrapin House, and availing himself of weeping-cherries and weeping-willows, Hanshichi proceeded up the street by fits and starts. Once the famous chandelier had been put behind, the quarter was very much like the Yoshiwara. The nature of the almost exclusively masculine throngs, by which he meant the scarcity of foreigners, had already given him the impression that the quarter, while masquerading as an accommodation for these last, was really a fruit of Japanese commercial enterprise aimed at a clientele almost certain to grow, Japanese who were curious about foreigners. These were, most of them, men who wanted to go home and tell envious friends about foreign whorehouses. Most of the things he saw as he moved up the street confirmed the impression.

Customer relations seemed to be managed in essentially the Yoshiwara fashion. Except for the cheapest houses, customers did not go directly to the places of their choice. They needed the mediation of teahouses, even when the places were well known and no mediation was necessary. Spreading work and money was a part of the system. Conspicuous among the feminine minority were comely women in modest but elegant dress who carried lanterns bearing the names of teahouses. They were, as the conventional expression had it, leading customers by the hands, even them who were not at all in need of being led.

And how did he know which were the cheapest houses? Well, as the old saying had it, most truthfully, they who knew, knew. Then there was the matter of the cages (so to speak) in which the cheaper places displayed their wares, as a cheap restaurant might have models of its menu on display. Rows of women sat behind lath screens, the laths so placed that pawing was not possible but visibility was not obstructed. Hanshichi had had enough experience to distinguish a woman of no quality from one who had some amount, and so had a notion of what the prices would be. Or he would have had, at any rate, in the Yoshiwara. Prices might be higher here, because of the nature of the presumed clientele. He was mildly distressed to find no really uncomely women awaiting incineration. They had been gathered from pleasure quarters in Edo and near-by provinces, and obviously the intention was to make a good impression on such foreigners as came calling.

A procession came by, giving evidence that the Yoshiwara class system was pertinent as well. A woman with attendants passed by on pattens so high that she required support to maintain her balance. She was grandly, heavily dressed and coifed, she had a walk so artificial, each step requiring crossed ankles, that it was almost a dance, albeit a very slow one, and she had male attendants to provide the support and ladies in waiting, more modestly accoutered, to emphasize her grandeur. An *oiran* of the highest rank among courtesans, she was on her way to a teahouse to welcome a particularly favored (and doubtless wealthy) client. Or such would have been the case in the Yoshiwara.

He had by now returned to Terrapin House.

From this house Matsu came dashing, as if in flight.

"Did you have a good time?"

"I was all business. You would have been proud of me. Did you see her?"

"The *oiran*? It would have been hard not to."

"She's the one."

"The what one?"

"The one the Englishman has gone crazy over. Want me to go talk to her?"

Emerging from Terrapin House more deliberately and with more dignity, Goro had joined them.

"Have you gone crazy yourself?" he said. He would not have said it to Hanshichi.

"That would be the best way to make him run if he has things to run from."

"And besides, talking to her would be like shouting at a woman upstairs."

"Everyone waits to see who comes back with one of them," said Goro.

"No son of Edo could turn forty without knowing that much." Hanshichi had in fact just turned forty. "Unless he was a little peculiar."

"All I meant was that it wouldn't be a good idea to be conspicuous. Sometimes maybe. Like when someone thinks he's more important than you. But not now."

"You know I've never had that experience. But of course you're right."

So they waited, quite some time. The procession moved slowly, if for no better reason than that every step took so long. They could see that the courtesan had no one under her wing (it would have had to be quite some distance under). Then, a bit later, a foreigner came up, looking somewhat out of countenance. He also looked somewhat unhealthy, Hanshichi thought, but two or three things about foreigners were that you could never tell how old they were or what they were thinking or how they were feeling. The figure was tall and thin. Almost anyone would have been uncomfortable to be the cynosure of so many eyes, but Hanshichi thought he looked bored and irritable.

"Just as I expected," said Goro.

"It's the man Lloyd?"

"The very. And guess who else is with us. Look over there."

Hanshichi looked in the direction indicated. He saw a number of Japanese men, on one of whom Western dress rested more easily than on most of his countrymen.

"The one that got fired?"

"The very."

"He looks like an intelligent young fellow. If that's the sort of thing a foreign company does to intelligent young fellows we should close the country again."

"Go ahead. Have a try."

Having no wish to argue, they laughed. But Hanshichi would not at all have minded having a try had there been the smallest chance of success.

"We'll get rid of them some day," he said again.

"Let's wait and see what happens. He's not here just for the fun of it."

"But it won't be good if someone recognizes us. We're occupying a space almost as conspicuous as the one they just occupied."

So they withdrew behind a profusely weepy willow, through which they could see but were not likely to be seen.

The Westernized Japanese went into Terrapin House a few minutes after the Englishman had gone in. He did it without the mediation of a teahouse. Perhaps he only meant to join one of the guided tours. This seemed unlikely. Probably he was an old and esteemed customer. This sort of behavior was marginally acceptable, but discouraged, because it had a corrosive effect on the system.

There was no call for them to feel out of place. The parade up and down the street consisted in large measure of rubberneckers or window shoppers. A stroll around the quarter, with pauses for each girl cage, was an inexpensive but interesting way for a fellow to pass an evening. Numbers of people were, like them, observing it all from the concealment of drooping branches. Hanshichi thought of Dr. Hepburn. Though there were no obvious missionaries among them, there could have been Japanese acolytes, for whom such pleasures were in theory proscribed.

The wait, though long, was not objectionably so, or boring. Hanshichi suggested that Matsu go have himself a good time; however, having been all business through so much of the evening, Matsu wished to go the whole distance.

Englishman and Japanese emerged together, and started towards the gate. They were having a warm conversation, entirely in a foreign language. Hanshichi would not have been able to say what language, though it was doubtful that they would be talking in anything other than the native language of one of the two. It soon became apparent that the warmth was not entirely friendly. Hanshichi wished that, extraterritoriality or no extraterritoriality, they had an interpreter. He could have wielded his authority to demand that the Japanese, at least, speak Japanese, but, in the circumstances, that would not have been the most prudent thing to do.

The warmth was beginning to attract attention. So the two went out through the gate. The marshlands beyond were dark. The soft light of paper lanterns, although the myriads of them on the main avenue rendered the quarter radiant, went only a very short distance beyond the gate. The two were so deeply engaged in their disagreement, whatever it might be, that they failed to notice the three who were following them.

The two seemed to be at increasingly cross purposes. Their voices rose.

A Japanese sentence suddenly intruded itself upon the dialogue: "Japanese are liars."

And the curtain of alien speech descended again. From time to time it opened, briefly, and the same sentence came forth. That the Englishman should know the Japanese word for Japanese was not surprising, and the verb was the commonest in the language, but that he should know the Japanese for "liars" did seem surprising. Hanshichi could only conclude that he had good reason to know and use it.

"It's English?" whispered Hanshichi.

"Yes."

"You've been here quite a while. Haven't you learned a little?"

"Very little. Very very little. It's about something the foreigner thinks is his and wants back. I don't know what it is. I think maybe he hasn't said. No need to say."

The two were now shouting. The Englishman swung on the Japanese, who dodged as if he had had experience.

Hanshichi and his companions now stepped forward. They pulled the Japanese away. He seemed ready to flee if only they would let him. The Englishman did flee. They made no attempt to pursue him. There was not much they could have done in any event, what with unequal treaties and consular courts and that sort of thing.

"So you're back in Yokohama," said Goro. "Why?"

"Pretty obvious, I'd think. There aren't many other reasons why a man would come to a place like this."

"You weren't in there long enough to accomplish much of anything. You came because he told you to. What was the argument about."

"What are arguments with foreigners always about?"

"I wouldn't know. I've never had one."

"All right. What are arguments between Japanese generally about?"

"Women."

"You're stupid even as people like you go."

The man had seen too much of foreigners, thought Hanshichi. What would things be like when a great many Japanese had associated with a great many foreigners?

"I'm sure I am," said Goro, amiably. He showed great promise, thought Hanshichi. "Tell me what I need to know."

"It doesn't matter whether they're Japanese or foreign. Men don't get into fights over whores."

"You must not see many plays."

"I don't see any. There are so many new things we have to learn, it's stupid to use up time on old things. Maybe we should just heave them all out. Then they wouldn't be a temptation."

The man had a point, thought Hanshichi. But we'll get rid of them all some day. He did not say it aloud this time.

"You must hear what the whole town is talking about."

"You mean Edo. I have nothing to do with Edo. What's the whole town talking about? This little town doesn't talk about much of anything but money."

"Oh, 'The Blood Bath at the Yoshiwara' among other things. That's about men fighting over a whore,"

"All right, have it your way. But we weren't arguing over a whore."

"And you were—?"

There was silence.

"I'd much appreciate an answer."

"I was waiting for you to finish."

"I asked what you were fighting about."

"Why didn't you say so?"

Yes, the man had seen too much of foreigners. No one in Edo had ever addressed Hanshichi in so sneering a manner.

"You can probably catch him," continued the man after a period of silence. "He's the one to ask. He's the one that was upset. I wasn't, not the least little bit. Take my pulse if you don't believe me."

Goro started off. Hanshichi and Matsu followed after.

"You're going to let him get by with it?" "Edo is Edo, Yokohama is Yokohama."

"Yokohama is still part of Japan. Or am I wrong?"

"It's a little hard to say. But what we do here mostly when foreigners are involved is let them have their way. The big thing is to keep them happy."

"This won't go on forever."

"Of course it won't. And the best way to make sure that it's over in a hurry is to be good little boys. Let's try and see where we are."

Physically they were back near the northern end of the causeway. Soon they would turn left along the avenue through the Japanese town.

"I've enjoyed our little night on the town."

"I can think of a thing or two that might have improved it," said Matsu.

"Nothing to keep you from coming back now that you know the way."

"Nothing except that I don't have the time or money. Minor details, I agree."

"I'll go back up to Edo tomorrow myself, but I'm thinking of leaving you here for a while. I don't suppose anyone would object?" he asked Goro.

"Not as long as it has to do with an Edo case. I don't suppose it would be a good idea to limit yourself to just one Yokohama case. That would be putting all your eggs in one basket."

"Doing what?"

"Oh. I must have picked up some English wisdom even if I haven't learned much English. I mean it's a good idea to spread your risks. The Lloyd case has possibilities, but it could turn out not be the right one."

"Was it the same man in all the cases involving the detached head?"

"We have no way of knowing. He was always masked. Besides, no one saw him more than once."

"And did he, or they, always sound like a good Edo man? No one could mistake the Lloyd person for that."

"They might know up in the magistrate's office. I don't."

"You'll have to spend some time in the magistrate's office, young fellow. Pull your rank on them."

"I don't have any."

"You work in Edo. You outrank them all."

"Not exactly what I would call the best possible attitude," said Goro.

"I was joking. How could anything so ridiculous be anything but a joke?"

The expression on Goro's face said that he wasn't sure.

"We must begin with a general introduction to the foreign settlement. Some of the foreigner are here to save us from damnation and cut off our legs. Your Dr. Hebon is one of them. Then there are the tramps. We can come back to them in a minute if you're interested. Most of don't have the brains for the sort of thing we're talking about. The ones that are in business are mostly two kinds, branches of companies in Hong Kong and Shanghai, and independents. We know pretty well what the branches are up to. In plenty of the other cases we can't be sure."

"Which is the one with all the pots and pans?"

"They all have pots and pans. They must think we've never learned to cook. They may be right. The biggest one is a branch of the biggest company in Hong Kong. You wouldn't have been interested in any but the biggest. You're from Edo."

"I apologize for my little joke. You must forget it."

"Oh, I have forgotten it, completely. You must remind me what it was. My stupid words only spoke a truth everyone knows about Edo, its people, etc. Where was I?"

"Pots and pans. Biggest company in Hong Kong. You hadn't yet come to the Thompson company, but I'm sure you would have by now if I hadn't interrupted. You're not one to waste a person's time."

"The Thompson business came directly from London. So it's one of the one's we aren't sure about."

"What sort of business is it? Or what sort does it pretend to be?"

"It calls itself a gentleman's tailor. But there aren't that many gentlemen needing tailors. It's true that more of them are English than anything else, but it's also true that too many places call themselves gentlemen's tailors. The next biggest number is American, and you never saw a sloppier bunch. Not one of them ever saw the inside of a gentleman's tailor's place."

"Have a look around, young fellow, and see if you see any gentlemen getting tailored. So what do you think it does do?"

"Change money. That's what most of them do. A lot of them anyway. We officers of the law mustn't exaggerate. There's lots of money in money."

"Maybe that's why he's so partial to pawnshops. If he is. Someone is, anyway. Tell me more."

"Well, there's gold and there's silver, see, and each has its price, and the two prices have to be right."

"How do you know when they're right."

"You ask the English, and if you don't do what they tell you, you lose all of one of them, I think it's the cheap one, but I'm not sure. I don't have much to do with gold and silver. Anyway we're losing all of one of them, I'm not sure which. They buy it here and sell it in Shanghai or somewhere at the rate the English set, and make heaps of money, and we lose all of whichever it is. I'm not sure why this is bad as long as we have the other, but it does seem to be. We frown on it. And it's what a lot of them are up to. It's probably what Thompson's up to. But he does have scissors and cloth and that sort of thing, to make it look like a tailoring place."

"And does he have tailors and that sort of thing?"

"We'll find out when he has a customer."

"Are there any barbers?"

"I don't think so. They must cut each other's hair, but as you can plainly see they don't do it very often. Why do you ask?"

"I must have foreign hair on my mind. What about the others, the ones besides the English? Not many of them come from Hong Kong. So where did they come from?"

"Mostly they're Americans. A few Dutch, up from Jagaimo, or whatever it's called. And then there are a couple of Frenchmen, up from somewhere and lots of Chinese, only they all work for someone else. They don't have any legal staus. They haven't gotten around to forcing an unequal treaty on us. What's a stampede to the goldfields?"

"I've never actually seen one, but I'd imagine it's pretty much what it says it is. Somebody finds gold and every one else comes stampeding."

"Why don't we have stampedes? We have goldfields."

"The people who already have it all take whatever is found, and so there's nothing to go stampeding for. Don't tell anyone I said so. I wouldn't want it on my record. I suppose your first question has to do with the stampede they've been having somewhere in America."

"Place with a funny name."

"They all have funny names."

"Anyway that's where most of them are from. The goldfields that are getting stampeded on. The ones that don't find any gold keep on going west. I suppose they couldn't think of any other direction to go. They're a pretty stupid lot, and a pretty conceited lot. The English and Dutch may think they're better than we are, but they don't go around shouting about it. The Americans do, shout and shout. Someone said, I don't know whether it's true or not, that it's because of all the Chinese coolies in the goldfields.

Americans are too stupid to tell a Chinese from a Japanese."

"Yes, that is pretty stupid, a fellow has to admit."

"But you can't rule them out just because they're stupid. They're smart enough to team up with brainy Japanese or Chinese. Like in the case of the winter butterfly. That was very brainy, and we finally sent a stupid American up before a consular court."

"What about the brainy Chinese or Japanese?"

"We never caught him, or her, or them. Probably went off into the country, and there's not much you can do when that happens. As you know as well as I do. They might as well be off in the goldfields."

"There is no such thing as a winter butterfly."

"Of course there isn't. That's the whole point. Or one of the whole points. Another is that Japanese all know this and Americans all don't. Americans are the stupidest people in the world when it comes to butterflies and things like that. So there had to be a Japanese behind it. It was a white butterfly and it flew at night. Another thing butterflies don't do."

"It can't have been a real butterfly."

"Of course it wasn't. But it looked like one, and people panicked. They thought it was a ghost. I've never quite understood why people are so afraid of ghosts. Japanese people. I don't know much about any others."

"You seem to know quite a lot about Americans."

"We can do without sarcasm."

Hanshichi only smiled.

"Anyway, a whole street would panic, and he could rob any house he wanted. The butterfly came out only on windy nights. So we guessed what it was. It had to be something like a kite. It turned out to be made of stiff silk, very light, maybe Chinese, too big for a butterfly, but people didn't notice at night. We caught it, and went to the other end of the string, and there was the American. He said he did it all by himself, but of course it wasn't true. He probably said it because he'd be sent up to a consular court and scolded, but a Japanese might get his head chopped off, and the game would be up."

"Why did you send him to the consulate if you knew he'd get off?"

"To warn Japanese, and maybe some Chinese too, not to team up with Americans. But whoever he was he got away. Maybe he was the same as the monkey man. The monkey man was pretty brainy too, and he made a pile of money, and got away. We caught the monkey, though, and the American. It was tricky. We had to identify the monkey and send it on its way without letting the American know. We could be fairly sure it wouldn't tell him, but you can't be really sure with monkeys. Have you ever tried to identify a smart monkey in the middle of the night?"

"Did the monkey get his head chopped off?"

"Of course. Our system of justice is completely fair. But it got a reprieve. It was a well-known monkey, and we hoped it would lead us to whoever was behind it."

"Where does the monkey population come in? Behind the Dutch and ahead of the French, maybe? I always say it's easier to tell monkeys apart than foreigners."

"It was a trained monkey," said Goro, not taking the question seriously. "An American pretended to be the trainer, but obviously he wasn't. Whoever was the trainer was a sly one. He never gave himself away. The monkey lived with the American. When it performed on the street the American pretended to be giving orders. But it had his eye on someone in the crowd. We never found out who it was, or how he, who knows, maybe she, gave commands. Maybe by batting an eye, or looking happy or unhappy. Monkeys are brainy little creatures."

"Like Japanese and Chinese."

"When we took the monkey and the American in, the trainer probably headed off for the provinces." Which was an oblique admission that Lord Tokugawa was not in complete control of the provinces."

"You haven't told us what this genius of a monkey did."

"No, I guess I haven't. It wasn't too different from what the winter butterfly did. It scared people. It would climb up on roofs and make noises and throw things. A monkey can make some pretty unfriendly noises when it wants too, and there are always things on a roof for anyone with energy and ambition to climb up and throw. So people would go out into the street, and get robbed, either the people themselves or the houses they left empty, depending on which looked best."

"Maybe a Japanese (or Chinese) had more than one American in his stable."

"We thought of that. But we'll probably never know."

"What do you make of all this, young fellow? Or is your heart still back in Terrapin House?"

"I didn't miss a thing. Or if I did I don't know what it was."

"That's fairly obvious. So what do you make of it?"

"Well, first of all, working in Yokohama might be pretty interesting. I'm not saying I'm going to leave Edo."

"I'm sure that as you gather knowledge and experience Edo will have reason to be very grateful. What else?"

"It's all very interesting, but I doubt that it has much to do with our case. It's basically very different. No one got robbed."

"Unless you think of extortion as robbery."

"But the pawnbrokers might get their money back."

"They won't, though."

"All right, they might, even if they won't. As a matter of fact I'm not sure—it's your fault if I'm saying things I shouldn't—why we're so interested in the case. Nobody has done anything so very bad. Are we in it just to show we can manage it? That's about the best reason I can think of."

"Number one: a foreigner is probably involved, which could mean war, which we don't much want (at this point). Number two: it's a good idea to have pawnbrokers think you care about them. You can never tell why you might need one. You agree, I suppose, that a foreigner might be involved?"

"How else do you explain the head?"

"And that the man who extorted money from the pawnbrokers was not foreign?"

"All we have to go on is the way he talked, and I don't know much about that. But yes, he probably was Japanese. So it's the opposite of the other two cases. A Japanese (or maybe a Chinese), or maybe a-couple of them, used a couple of stupid Americans to do the dirty work and get caught. In our case there had to be a foreigner there somewhere. Where else could the head have come from?"

"You think the foreigner provided his own head? The case of the headless foreigner."

Matsu fell into a pout.

"There is a possibility you don't seem to have thought of," said Goro. "The Dutch have been around quite a while. And everybody says they're very good at languages. One of them might have picked up Japanese well enough to pass as a Japanese."

"From what you've said, the chances that it was a stupid American are pretty poor. For other reasons the chances that it's a Frenchman are. So it should be a Dutchman or an Englishman we're after. Or maybe a Chinese, but I sort of doubt it. He'd have as much trouble as a Japanese finding a pink head with red hair growing all over it. Are you listening, young fellow? I'm sorry if I hurt your feelings. Sometimes I'm too witty for my own good."

Matsu managed a smile and a nod.

"So you stay in Yokohama a while and see what you can see. And it might be a good idea to take along someone who knows a little English. You don't work in Yokohama. So you won't lose any face."

"And I won't make many points either."

"You're wrong there. You'll be completely on your own down here. Unless something has slipped my memory, it will be the first time. Make a good thing of it and you might have a chance to overthrow me."

"Don't mention it." Which was a way of saying that this was unthinkable.

The next morning, before Hanshichi started back for Edo, the three of them had another stroll through the foreign settlement. Hanshichi was pleased to see that he was already rather good at identifying the varieties of foreigners, and at distinguishing between the two broad varieties of English firms. The English were dour and haughty, the Dutch were fat and jolly, the Americans were dirty. The French did not show themselves. Of course Hanshichi had only Goro to tell him whether he was right or not, and Goro had his prejudices. Hanshichi was rather confident in the matter of the two English varieties. The Shanghai and Hong Kong firms were doing a brisk retail business in both directions. The others did not seem to be doing much business of any kind. Hanshichi looked in again on the bazaar where he had bought his gifts. He bought a watch.

The Thompson company did not reveal much about itself. It was among those that did not seem to be doing much of anything. The Hong Kong and Shanghai places were somewhat open, the others very closed. The sign at the Thompson gate invited tailoring customers in two languages. Otherwise it was very uninviting.

"I don't have any money," said Matsu, in good spirits once more.

"That's part of our business," said Hanshichi, giving him some.

# 4

"Keep in touch," said Hanshichi, leaving Matsu and Goro at the inn. This meant sending a runner when there was anything to report. The runner was the only means of rapid communication over considerable distances, and he was not so very rapid, even when he did in fact run. "And don't lose sight of the opportunities that are opening before you."

"I'll be all business."

"That isn't what I said or meant."

Hanshichi thought that he would have a leisurely stroll back to Edo, with a drink at this and that spot famous for cherry blossoms. When cherry blossoms fall, however, they fall (like a guillotine) rapidly. Such cherry trees as he passed already had the ragged look of summer. He did stop for a drink at each of the two post stations along the way, because that was what the lone traveler did, blossoms or none. He could have had the attentions for an hour or two of one of the waitresses to be found at each station, but he had not been married for long, and was still somewhat monogamous. He was back in Kanda before dark.

He did not get much sleep. There was a fire in the night. It was not much of a fire as Edo fires went, only five or six houses, but in Edo a person could never be sure. The whole city might go up in flames. It did from time to time. With as many possessions as they could carry done up in kerchiefs, he and Sen, his wife, went outside and took the measure of the situation. The fire was upwind from them. So sleep was out of the question. Little fire carts sped past, with ridiculously small hoses dangling from them. Hanshichi knew, as did everyone in Edo, that their function was not to extinguish fires. It was to protect the firemen, amateurs all of them, who tore down houses in the path of a fire.

There was no part of Kanda in which Hanshichi did not have friends. When it became apparent that Sen could undo the kerchiefs, he went, as good manners asked, to make inquiries about people who might have incurred losses. It was still dark when he came back. He went off to a bathhouse and after his morning bath turned to his breakfast. He had not yet finished, and dawn was just coming over the sky, when a runner came from the constable over by the river. This person was Hanshichi's immediate superior, though not the only such person at whose beck and call he was. Hanshichi's presence was required immediately. It would not have occurred to him to complain. This sort of thing happened all the time and was part of his business. Early morning after a fire in the night was not the best possible time for it to happen, but then.

He set out immediately. In the constable's parlor was a man immediately recognizable, by his coiffure and by his imperious bearing, as of the military aristocracy. Hanshichi, as has been noted, preferred to have nothing to do with the aristocracy. He could not, however, walk out on a guest of the constable's.

The man's bearing may have been imperious, for that was a part of him which he could not shake off, but his speech was mild and courteous.

He told about himself. He lived in, and had so early in the morning come from, a district west of the castle which suggested him to belong to the petty aristocracy, as Hanshichi called it. This did indeed prove to be the case. Petty aristocracy was still aristocracy, thought Hanshichi, trying not to look rueful. The man's name was Nakajima, and he was in the service of a family named Sugita, in direct attendance upon the shogun.

"What I am going to tell you must be absolutely secret. I have already told the constable. and he thought it best to call you. No one in the house knows that I have come. I have come without orders or permission. I could be in trouble if word gets back to anyone in the house. Others might be in even worse trouble. And the Sugita family might be embarrassed and dishonored. That would be the worst thing. Do I have your word that this is in complete confidence?"

Hanshichi hoped to die if he let so much as a word slip forth. "I am very good at keeping secrets," he added. Indeed he was far better than his sister, who had come to him with the secret of the alien head.

The only member of the youngest Sugita generation, a boy upon whom the family hopes rested, had disappeared. The constable had called Hanshichi because it was near a Confucian temple on the edge of Kanda, near Hanshichi's abode, that the Sugita heir, an adolescent, had disappeared. With two attendants, he was on his way to the temple for an examination in the Chinese classics. Among the initiation rites for young aristocrats was passing the examination, held regularly at the temple. Each of the examinees was required to read, and if asked comment upon, a passage from the classics. The text was in Chinese, and the examinee did not know which passage would be chosen for him to come to terms with. It was a difficult and important examination.

As soon as the disappearance became known, the family informed the temple that he had fallen ill. The truth could be troublesome. It was not impossible that the boy would be asked to kill himself if it came to seem that he had run away. Numbers of men had searched all through the city during the week that had intervened. They had found no trace of him. So Nakajima had come to the constable. In a sense it had been insubordinate of him to do so, but he was sure that the constable and Hanshichi would see that had only the interest of the family in mind.

"And when and how, exactly, did he disappear?"

The three had set out in darkness, for examinees were required to be at the temple hours in advance. The Sugita residence lay very near the outer moat of Edo Castle. They walked north and east along the moat and along the Kanda River, which fed it. The temple lay to the north of the river. They had only a lantern to light the way. The temple had come into sight, dimly and darkly, ahead of them.

"One of the men with him slipped and broke the thong of a sandal. The other held the lantern close while he fixed it. This took some time. When they were ready to go on the boy had disappeared. No one could blame the man for slipping. Paths get wet at night. But they should have kept an eye on the boy."

"Would there be any reason for him to run away?"

"None that we can think of. He's a healthy, good-natured boy, and he was one of the best students at the academy, maybe the very best. He had nothing to be afraid of. It may be that he's a little too handsome for his own good."

"A prize for someone to walk off with. A little far-fetched, but not impossible. You've said nothing about ransom. So I suppose there has been no ransom note?"

"I wouldn't be here if there had been."

"We're sorry to have troubled you." This was Hanshichi, who was not as directly subject to reprisals as the constable. He quite took over the interview.

"I sometimes forget myself. No, there has been nothing about ransom."

"He's a little young for a woman to be chasing after. Not for a man, maybe. We can't dismiss any possibility. Have any others come to you through the long lonely days of searching? Any other possibilities, I mean."

"Only one that's even more far-fetched. I hesitate to speak of it."

"We can't dismiss any possibility that is a possibility. As I have so wisely stated."

"It's a woman's idea. The sort no man is supposed to allow inside his head."

"That may be true of you up there on top, but we ordinary people love silly ideas. I start most of my days with one or more, and sometimes they turn out to be pretty good ones."

Hanshichi hoped that this was encouraging, but maybe it was merely garrulous. The silence continued for a time.

"Well, women's idea or not, some of us have been victims of it. They laugh when they speak of it, but it isn't very funny. The idea is that he's been spirited off. You've heard, I'm sure, of people being spirited off."

The idea being a popular one of the time, both Hanshichi and the constable had of course heard of it.

The word Nakajima used in fact contained two spirits. It meant something like being spirited off by a spirit. It referred to a supernatural event.

"You wouldn't have come here if you believed that. I'm not saying that it never happens or that you're a fool for taking it seriously. But if that's what happened there's nothing to do but wait. He'll be back one of these days, and when he comes back he'll say he doesn't know what happened. Someone with a big nose took him off in a big hurry, the way an eagle might. He doesn't know where he was or who took him there, and then just like that he's back again where it all started." There were no pronouns in Hanshichi's statement. So it could have applied to man or woman. "If people are foolish enough to believe it, well, they deserve to be taken in. Remember I've given it as my view that you don't believe a word of it. In most cases I've heard of someone who doesn't have enough of something goes off having his fill of it, and then he comes back and says he has no idea what happened. But this is a young boy, and you say he's healthy and happy. What would he be off getting his fill of?"

"Of course I don't believe it. I shouldn't even have mentioned it. But I didn't want to keep anything back. I'd say that it's the most popular theory at the moment."

"It isn't impossible. But a person wonders. Why do we hear of so many cases now when we didn't use to hear of any at all? It's something about the mood of the times. People are nervous and a little unbalanced maybe. Especially in Edo, with all that talk of bringing the Kyoto people back. Maybe I shouldn't mention it, but it's there, and Edo won't be anything without the shogun." Hanshichi now addressed the constable. "I'll have to tell you about my trip down to Yokohama some time. There's plenty to be nervous about. This country will never be the same. Which is fine if you don't want it to be the same. Myself, I do."

"It may be that we're a little more unbalanced than most," said Nakajima. "You've heard about our curse?"

"You're very own curse?" Neither Hanshichi nor the constable remembered having heard of it.

"Our very own curse. We live in Morning-glory House. I'm sure you've heard about that."

"I have indeed," said Hanshichi. The constable nodded. "Probably I once knew the name of the owner, but I'd forgotten. I forget things. You mustn't take it as anything personal."

Nakajima laughed. Hanshichi had not meant to be funny, but an unintentional joke could do as well as an intentional one.

"Let's make sure we have it right about the curse," said the constable. "It could be important. People make curses work whether they want to work or not."

"That part of town is full of haunted houses. The ghosts are all women who died violent deaths. They either killed themselves or got murdered. Ours is called a haunted house. I don't think anyone has seen a ghost, but it fits the pattern. I don't remember how many generations back it was, but quite a few, a Sugita man killed one of his women. The morning-glory thing is her revenge. Or so they say. She was wearing a summer kimono with a morning-glory pattern when she was killed. Whenever a morning-glory blooms on the grounds something terrible happens to someone in the family. So they say. All through the winter and into the fall gardeners and maids go over the grounds pulling up anything that might be a morning-glory. Even so one gets through now and then. A white one did it last summer."

Hanshichi made bold to speak of the obvious. "It seems just a bit odd that you didn't mention this before."

"Well, in the first place, it's all nonsense."

"Not many things in this business can be dismissed as nonsense."

"In the second place, I assumed you knew. Everyone seems to know. It's a great embarrassment for the Sugita family."

"Everyone may know the story, but not everyone associates it with a family named Sugita."

"In the third place, even if the curse was at work, it doesn't tell us anything about how the boy disappeared and where he is."

"I don't think we need to make such a big thing of it," said the constable. "It was an innocent oversight."

"One oversight leads another," said Hanshichi. "And so on."

"If you have these doubts," said Nakajima, "it might be wiser for you not to take on the case."

"Not at all," said Hanshichi. "It's the sort of thing that keeps a fellow on his toes. I have a good idea of where it happened. I'll have a look, and maybe afterwards I'll go have a look around Number Four." Number Four was the part of the castle grounds in which the Sugita mansion lay.

"If anyone asks why you're there, make something up. People see the famous Hanshichi nosing around and they wonder why. Let me say again that word of what has happened must not get out."

"Maybe I should wear a mask."

"Not the best way, I'd say, of avoiding attention."

They all laughed, and parted on amiable terms. The petty aristocracy, Hanshichi had always thought, was really the very worst kind, but this man seemed an exception. Perhaps his master was not a bad sort either. In many a family like the Sugitas many a head would have rolled and many a belly been ripped open at the disappearance, quite possibly through carelessness, of an only son. None seemed to have done so in this case.

In the afternoon Hanshichi did as he had said he would do. He took in reverse the walk that the three had taken. He did not expect to find much, and he did not. All along the north bank of the Kanda River to the bridge by which the three had crossed he examined the path for signs that someone had slipped and fallen. He would have been happier if he had come upon such, but he was not greatly disappointed at finding none. A week and more had passed, and, except perhaps in winter, Edo almost never went a week without rain. The stretch of the river along which the incident had occurred was known as "tea water," signifying that it was clean enough for steeping a cup of tea. It did look reasonably clean, but a great many people lived along it, and they had no sewers. Hanshichi would have preferred to go to an aqueduct for his tea water.

He walked along the north bank to a point just beyond which its flow was from the north rather than the west and from which some of its waters proceeded southwards through a tunnel to provide moats for the protection of Lord Tokugawa. The bridge on which he recrossed the river was guarded, for to the north lay a mansion of a branch of the Tokugawa clan. Hanshichi, as we have seen, had little regard for or interest in the aristocracy, but this was the least affluent and most rebellious of the Tokugawa houses. He did allow himself a mild interest in these unruly Tokugawa adolescents. The bridge was guarded, chiefly, it seemed, against possible intruders from the direction of the castle. Though he did not look at the guard, he was sure that he was being glared at.

He was no longer sure, on the south side of the river, that he was following the precise route of the three. It did not matter a great deal. Nothing untoward had been reported from this sector. He first walked through untamed lands that had somewhat the look of the primeval Musashi Plain. Then he was in lands where dwelt the aristocracy, not the one in attendance upon His Majesty, for that had stayed with him in Kyoto, but the more recent military one, petty and otherwise, in more or less direct attendance upon Lord Tokugawa. He sometimes wondered why Japan needed more than one aristocracy, since the one with which he was on more intimate terms in Edo was quite objectionable enough for one narrow country; but he would not have voiced the doubt even if he had had someone to receive it.

In a general way he walked along three sides of a rectangle. If he had walked directly west from Kanda the route would have been much shorter, but his object was not to save time and steps. He would quickly have departed the Kanda flatlands and encountered hills. He would have had no bridges or barriers or surly guards to contend with, but he would have been aware of crossing a divide all the same. The regions west of the castle were very different from his eastern ones. They had fewer streets and far fewer pedestrians, and far more walls.

This was indeed a walled-in place. People in his own mercantile quarter did not live out in the open. They had barriers between themselves and the elements, barriers that could be removed in sticky seasons to permit the passage through of the elements, but barriers all the same. Beyond these were, uniformly, decorative plants, especially, in this season, morning glories. In these aristocratic districts plants were walled in, for the enjoyment of those within and not for the whole world as it passed by. The walls were not displeasing. They were of pleasant, soft, neutral tones, wood and plaster. Many of the walls had long houses along them, quarters for servants and guards and the like. The windows were uniformly enclosed in weathered wood, the color of Edo itself. Hanshichi could not have objected on aesthetic grounds. Yet there was something chilling about these streets. He liked having plants to brush against, and few lanes and alleys in the mercantile quarters were without them.

Hanshichi wished briefly that he had declined to have anything to do with the case. He did not feel at home, and he did not like the class to which the inhabitants belonged. In his own Kanda he could not have walked a block, and the blocks were much smaller there than here, without running into someone he knew. He did not expect that to be true here. The more people he knew and stopped for a talk with the better were his chances of coming upon something interesting. Chance encounters and random tips were very important in his business.

He had no trouble finding the house of the morning-glory curse. There was nothing distinctive about it. The walls were plaster and topped with tiles like all the others up and down the streets and the front wall had a long-house within. Several men emerged as he was having a casual stroll (at any rate he hoped that he made it look casual) past the wall. One or both of the men in attendance on the Sugita boy might have been among them. He had no way to identify them. Back in Kanda it would have been easy.

The house and grounds seemed to be expansive, suggesting that the Sugita family had a certain eminence. It had been Hanshichi's experience that the pettiest aristocrats were the nastiest, and there had been those indications that the head of the family was a reasonably magnanimous and forgiving man. But Hanshichi would have had trouble evading questions about the source of his information, and he had made those promises of secrecy.

He stood for a time at a corner of the Sugita property and wondered what to do next. Have a drink—that seemed a good idea. It was a time of the afternoon when he would not be embarrassed to be seen drinking. There were mercantile districts a little north and a little south of the property, and no mercantile quarter was without its drinking quarters. They were frequented mostly by the lower orders, people who made deliveries to and did menial work for the upper orders, and they were the establishments in this part of town in which he felt most nearly at home. He might run into someone he knew, and striking up a conversation with even a stranger could do no harm. Gossip was important in his business. It had been his experience that gossip was rarely without some measure of foundation.

He went north, because that would be on is way home if he decided that he had done enough for one day. He found a little establishment and took a seat in a corner.

When he had his drink he surveyed the prospect. Business was surprisingly good for the time of day. Perhaps the rest of the clientele were like him. He felt at home in places like this.

He saw a face that he recognized. It was a woman's face and not a pretty one. The wide mouth and the small eyes made him think of a frog. Though not by any standard a pretty face, it had its own homely charm.

"Roku. It's good to see you. I was beginning to think I didn't know anybody, and that would have been embarrassing. May I join you?"

"It would be an honor, really too much of an honor." She motioned to a cushion beside her on the matted floor. "What brings you here? I wouldn't have thought of this as your part of town. I doubt that anyone would."

"Oh, something high-class turns up from time to time, if you're patient. And what brings you here?"

He knew perfectly well. She too was from Kanda, and he knew all about her.

"Business, business."

Not the most interesting answer possible, but a straightforward one. She knew that he knew what her business was. The hamper that was the mark of it was on the floor beside her. She frequented the high-class houses and purveyed cold meals to the employees, especially the lesser ones. Many were bachelors, and for this reason and that it was often inconvenient for them to get their own meals, even cold ones, or to go out. Such women generally had a more profitable stock in trade: themselves. She might not be the most alluring sexual object imaginable, but many a lowly samurai type was starved for any such object.

"So what do you hear about the affairs of the swells?"

"Oh, they're all hoping they can send their families back to the sticks one of these days."

This was a reference to the growing inability of the shogunate to control its barons. They had been required to keep their families in Edo, hostages in effect, and the time seemed at hand when they might not be.

"Do you think it will happen?"

"Everyone else seems to think so, and that's what's important."

"Do you hear of any missing people?"

"Oh, just the usual sort of thing, and they're not missing for long. Wife found in a well. Wife found chewed up in the kennels. Wife found burned beyond recognition. Makes a girl grateful to be a nobody."

"Do you know of the Sugita house up there?"

"Who doesn't?"

"Do you do any business there?"

"Wouldn't dream of it."

"Why?"

"You don't know? It's a haunted house. That's why everyone knows about it, and if you don't you must be the only person this side of the castle that doesn't." Her sweeping gesture covered everything between China and America via the North Pole.

"I meant why wouldn't you dream of it. Nothing will happen to you if you watch out for morning-glories."

"And how do you advise me to do that?"

"I suppose what I mean is that it doesn't seem to be a very

spooky kind of spook. It doesn't come creeping up on you with no feet in the middle of the night."

"I just don't like haunted houses."

"And I suppose you've known a great many of them."

"I'll let that one pass because you're everybody's Hanshichi, the person to go to when you're in trouble. But I'll tell you someone who doesn't care whether it's haunted or not. That's Yasu. She's in and out all the time and seems to have good customers."

"Has she found out anything unusual about the place?"

"Only that they're very big eaters and therefore very good customers. And they found a morning-glory there last summer. Isn't that the silliest thing you ever heard of?"

"I thought you were the one that believed in that sort of thing."

"Well I sort of do and sort of don't, and when anyone tells me to go into the morning-glory house, not that you actually did, I sort of do. Well now, that's very generous of you."

Hanshichi was paying for the drinks, all of which were rice products. Yokohama may have heard of beer, whiskey, wine, etc., but the plebeian parts of Edo had not.

"I'd like to meet Yasu."

Yasu was Roku's best friend, a more comely girl in the same business.

"You have met her. The snaggle-toothed one."

This did not make Yasu sound very pretty, but in fact she was. He was sure that if he had used the same adjective Roku would have demurred and pointed out how very pretty she was.

"Of course I've met her. What I meant was I'd like to see her. Could you arrange something?"

"She should be in his part of town somewhere. Will you be around for a while?"

"Yes."

He did not know what she meant by "a while," and if he was no longer on this very spot when she came back with Yasu no one would be greatly inconvenienced.

She went out. He stayed behind for a time.

It struck him as interesting that the prettier and more feminine of the two women did not share the other's fear of the supernatural. Quite possibly she was afraid but frequented the morning-glory house all the same. If so she placed a high value upon her customers there, and from this it might follow that she knew a thing or two about them.

He did not stay long. Though he liked to drink, he was not really a good drinker, and too much drink in the middle of the day had been known to lead to indiscretion. An attentive waitress, attentive both to him and to the interests of the shop, kept refilling his cup. When the flagon was empty it would be difficult not to order another. She would start bringing him cups of tea by way of reminder.

When the flagon was empty he paid his bill and went out.

Not sure what to do next, and sure that something would come up—something usually did, and he was doing as well as he usually did at the beginning of a case—he made another pass at the house of the morning-glories. He was at the end of the front wall and about to turn a corner when two men came out. One of them had come out when last he passed. He seemed to go in and out with some frequency. Instead of turning the corner Hanshichi reversed himself and went again past the front wall.

The two were in heated discussion. They seemed to disagree about something important. Hanshichi was in a better position to eavesdrop than on that evening in Yokohama. He knew the language. He did not, however, have darkness and a weeping-cherry for concealment. As he walked past, one of the two was saying that this was not the time and place. What time and place did he suggest, then, said the other, his manner indicating most clearly that speed was of the essence. Perhaps the first recognized Hanshichi, whose face was known by a great many people with something to hide. He did not answer until Hanshichi was out of earshot.

Hanshichi turned the corner at the other end of the front wall, and then another, and he saw Roku and her friend Yasu coming towards him. Yasu was prettier than ever, he thought. Some girls bloomed early and faded, some were a long time in blooming, some did not bloom at all, and some were in bloom most of their lives. Yasu's prettiness seemed an honest representation of the bone structure beneath, and likely to last. He would not at all mind buying an afternoon snack from her, should the occasion arise. Roku, though a cheerful and friendly girl, did not look as if her afternoon snacks would be as tasty.

"What luck," said Hanshichi. "And what a pretty pink you are. Like a lotus in the full bloom of summer."

Roku counted on her fingers. "If it had the right number of syllables it would be a *haiku*. Pink, maybe. But pretty?"

Yasu only smiled, a very pretty smile, even prettier, perhaps, by virtue of being somewhat snaggle-toothed.

"If we hurry they may still be there."

The women asked no questions, and hurried. What was important to Hanshichi was important to them. They hurried up to the corner of the Sugita property, and Hanshichi peeked around. The two men were still there, and still engaged in warm, possibly angry conversation.

"Who are they?"

"One of them is Matazo. They're talking about money."

Hanshichi was pleased though not especially surprised at the name. Matazo was one of the men who had been in attendance on the vanished Sugita boy.

"You can read lips?"

"No. But that's what they're talking about. Matazo needs it and doesn't have it. The other one, forget his name, has plenty and doesn't need much. So what else could they be fussing about?"

"Fussing is the word, all right. Why does he need money?"

"Does it matter? He needs it."

"Yasu is one of he reasons he needs it. She should know."

"Well, we are pretty good friends, that much is true. Let me just think a minute. I had a way of remembering the other one's name. What was it? I don't know him very well. He doesn't seem to like me."

"Maybe that's why he has so much money," said Roku. Yasu did not seem to hear.

"Heisuke, maybe?" suggested Hanshichi.

Heisuke was the name of the other attendant.

"That's it. Sukebei turned around. That's the way I remembered it, only I forgot. That's it exactly."

The two names were both written with two characters. Reverse the two for Heisuke and they became Sukebei, a name which no man actually bore, and which signified lewdness.

'Lots of money and the opposite of *sukebei*," mused Roku. "We might get on pretty well. Introduce us."

"But you refuse to go inside morning-glory house," said Hanshichi.

"I haven't gone inside, is more like what I said."

Hanshichi thought that he was doing fairly well, even though he seemed no closer to finding the Sugita boy. It could do no harm and might well do an amount of good to have a female attached to each of the men, but to say so might produce an adverse reaction. He always carried an amount of money and had a supply of good gift paper in the breast of his kimono, for just such occasions. One did not give naked money. It was the worst of rudenesses. He wrapped some coins, neither too minor nor too major, in each of two lengths of paper, and gave one to each of the women. This was to tell them that he would be grateful for whatever help they might be with the case. He was sure they would understand. Such women had a sense for such things. Of course he had not told them what the case was. But they would see the point. One of them was to keep close watch on the man with whom she was intimate, and if the other made some sort of arrangement with the other man, so much the better. They both knew what Hanshichi's work was, and knew that cooperation was expected and proper, and did not constitute deceit or betrayal.

Hanshichi did not think he would venture anything further today. It was broad daylight, and he did not want to attract attention. He told the women that he would hope to see them again soon, and he meant it. If a bit of infidelity to his wife Sen was called for, what she did not know would not hurt her, and if she found out about it she would understand.

He had another stroll past the Sugita gate.

"I need it and I need it quick," Matazo was saying. "Summer is almost here. And you promised."

"Not in writing."

Matazo's hand went to the hilt of his sword. In theory only men of the military class carried swords, but plenty of others did too. If he had drawn it Hanshichi would have intervened, even if they were of the military class and therefore above his jurisdiction. Matazo restrained himself, however. Hanshichi walked on.

Given what Hanshichi had learned of the circumstances of the two men, the "it" most probably indicated money. And why would the man need money specifically because of the advent of summer? One needed not more but less food and shelter in summer than in the other seasons, but, especially if one was a woman, new and different garments were needed. Yasu was definitely someone to cultivate.

Hanshichi went home. He had other cases, and the morning-glory house one could rest for a while. It was only rarely that he had only one case on his hands, and almost never that he had none at all. Edo was a well-behaved city, but this fact did not mean that everyone in it was well behaved all the time. Spring was an especially busy time. Saps were rising in the trees and grasses and also in the populace, and the effect of the rising was especially marked on young men, the most disorderly element in any city and society.

He had not expected quick news of developments in the case of the severed head, and there was none. It would be a pity if Matsu had no fun at all in Yokohama, but Hanshichi trusted him to not to have too much of it. There was no word from him.

Then, one evening, Matsu himself appeared. He had walked up from Yokohama that day, and come to Hanshichi's abode without stopping first at his own.

Hanshichi was having a nap. He had put in a strenuous day on the case of the weird dancing mistress. In a city like Edo, almost without vehicles, a person in the detective business had to be a good walker. For Hanshichi the day had been one of unusual distances on foot. He had made several trips to the river and back.

He would not be pampering himself if he had a nap.

Matsu said that he would wait, but Hanshichi heard voices and came out to the parlor. Sen had already poured tea.

"Case solved?"

"Not much farther along than when you last saw it. No more hair, no more heads. But there doesn't seem much more to do down there. Later maybe. Not now."

"I hope you enjoyed yourself."

"It's a nice place to visit, but I wouldn't want to live there."

"If you're finished with the case I'm finished with you."

"I said there's nothing more to be done down there. Doesn't that suggest that there's something to be done up here? That's what it would suggest to me, and you're much smarter than I am."

"Don't you have a sense of humor?"

"Ha ha." But the expression on his face said that it had not been a very good joke.

"I suppose the Japanese we saw arguing with the Englishman that night what was his name—

"Lloyd."

"—has come back to Edo."

"He hasn't been sighted since that night. Edo would be the obvious place for him to come back to. Have there been any new cases that he or whoever it is might have anything to do with?"

"I'll have to ask my sister only she's still busy with the cherry blossoms."

"There aren't any between here and Yokohama. Are there here?"

"Of course not. But that doesn't bother my sister."

"Anyway, there hasn't been any sight of him in the quarter."

"Where you've been spending your waking hours, and some sleeping ones too."

"Ha ha. I've asked the magistrate's office to watch. It isn't very friendly or very dependable, but it wouldn't want to be caught with its pants down. As the Americans say. The Englishman doesn't seem to be going to the quarter either."

"Maybe he's tired of it."

"Not likely. He's a genuine *sukebei*. If he's tired of the quarter he's tired of Japan, and I'm sure they'd be glad to send him home if he asked. He's out of money. His source of money was the man Saburo. I don't know why or how. That's one of the things I have to hunt him up and ask."

"Poor fellow."

"Why?"

"I meant you. There are probably as many Saburos as all the rest put together."

"It doesn't make things any easier, certainly."

"No family name?"

"You know the answer to that one. Excuse me. That wasn't polite. He called himself Tanaka when he worked for the Thompson place, but that doesn't mean anything. A foreign company wouldn't hire him if he didn't have a family name, so he picked up one that was lying around waiting to be picked up."

"Tough luck both ways."

By this Hanshichi meant that even as Saburo was the commonest of masculine given names, Tanaka was one of the commonest of family names. So Matsu had his work cut out for him. Hanshichi had known the answer that led to the retort for which Matsu apologized. Commoners were not supposed to have family names, and in humble, traditional places such as the regions east of the Sumida in Edo they did not. The Saburo in question might have been identified more specifically as Saburo the green grocer's boy or the Saburo from beside the bridge, but as to that Matsu knew nothing. If there existed such an epithet, it had not been a part of Saburo's life with Thompson and Lloyd in Yokohama. Hanshichi thought he knew why Saburo, which meant Third Son, was such a common given name. Parents of a first son and even a second son would try to think of something distinctive, but in the case of a third son they would be strongly inclined to say what the hell and just call him Saburo.

"So you're going to try and hunt him up. How?"

"A lot of footwork at first. I'll go around asking for Saburo, and when I find one I'll go have a look. It was dark, but I have a good idea what he looked like. And if that doesn't work I'll have to do some reading. I won't enjoy it. I'm better at footwork than at reading. But that's all right."

Neither Hanshichi nor Matsu was illiterate. Elementary education was widespread in Edo. Hanshichi did not ask for details about the reading. Most probably it would occur in Buddhist temples, where family records were kept.

"Good. You've thought it through."

Matsu was pleased. He did not this time say ha ha.

"And," continued Hanshichi, "I hope you remember Goro's advice."

"Well enough that you don't have to make yourself clearer. He said not to put all my eggs in one basket. I haven't."

"So you must be chock full of interesting stories."

"Yokohama is a pretty interesting place. But it's a lawless place. I wouldn't want to live there."

"As you have observed before."

"A thing about me is that I sometimes repeat myself. I don't suppose anyone else does. It's lawless because it's under two sets of laws and not under any at all. The magistrate is afraid to do anything and the consulates are too lazy to."

"What could the magistrate do?"

"Oh, arrest a few people, for a starter. He'd have to turn them over to the consulates, but that needn't keep him from arresting them. Funny how often women are involved in these things."

"Maybe not so funny. Put ten men and one woman on an island, and the woman is going to be involved in everything."

"There aren't many foreign women in the town, but one of them was involved in a case I thought might be the sort of thing we are after. She was an English woman."

"And you decided it wasn't?"

"It might be nearer the point to say I hoped it wasn't. There wasn't a thing I could have done about it. This English woman's husband was murdered. Everyone at the magistrate's office thought she did it, but no one saw the corpse, or had a chance to ask any questions. Everyone who knew her said she was a very nice woman, pretty and quiet and hard-working. And her husband liked Japanese women, and told her that she could go home if she didn't like it that he liked them. The poor woman really had no home to go to. I feel sort of sorry for her. I've never met her, of course."

"She was a nice woman. She isn't any more?"

"She may be a nice woman somewhere, but not in Yokohama. They shipped her back to England. The consulate did. They took one look at the corpse and sealed the coffin and sent it back to England too. Can't help wondering whether it's head went with it. With both of them gone and the consul the only one that knows much of anything, what can anyone do?"

"Have there been any other attractive murders?"

"Not that the magistrate knows about. There have been disappearances, but they could just have been sent home. Like the pretty widow. The magistrate's office knows only what the consulates tell it, and the consulates are lazy and bossy. It's a bad combination. Wouldn't you agree?"

"I only hope that you go on thinking it through all the rest of your days."

"It would be hard to get rid of a foreign corpse, with everyone watching."

"Is everyone?"

"The farmers and fishermen all know that if they want to live a while longer they'd better keep their eyes open. The magistrate finds a foreign corpse in your field or on your beach before you do and you're finished."

"So you think the case of Lloyd and Saburo is the best one to go after?"

"At least one foreigner and one Japanese have to be involved, the foreigner to provide the head, wherever he got it, the Japanese to go around using it on pawnbrokers. The Lloyd-Saburo combination is just right."

"The head could have come from a ship."

"I thought of that. But the customs inspectors are all Japanese. They don't set the rates and they don't control the operations, but they're the ones a head would have to get past. What I said about the farmers and fishermen I could say about them too. Let the magistrate find a head you've passed and you're finished."

"Remember the stories Sangoro told us?"

"The one about the monkey and the one about the butterfly. Of course."

"They both involved a Japanese and a foreigner working together. There must be plenty of cases like them."

"But the case of the foreign head is different. We can't be sure whoever provided the head knows what it's being used for. The Americans knew exactly what the monkey and the butterfly were being used for."

"So?"

"So it's not an American."

"A few days in Yokohama have made you a real expert."

"They've given me a feeling that not all foreigners are alike. I think we're more alike than they are."

"Good for us. We can play them off against each other and get rid of them all."

"Oh, as to that."

"Yes?"

"As to that. We'll see whether I'm right or not. Americans are mostly loners."

"The ones Sangoro told us about are the rare exceptions?"

"Most Americans sit right out in broad daylight and cheat you. They move things around in ways you can't possibly follow and they make things appear from nowhere. When it comes to picking a pocket no one in the world does it better than us Japanese. But when it comes to cheating right out there for everyone to see we have a lot to learn. You have to sort of admire them. And think that anyone who lets himself get cheated deserves to be cheated."

"Not the sort of remark a person expects from an officer of the law. I'll pretend I never heard it. I'd say you've been doing your work pretty well. I'll make sure the constable hears about it. Let's talk about cheerful things."

"I went to the foreign cemetery one afternoon."

"I was thinking more of the quarter in the evening. But let's hear about the cemetery. Maybe afterwards about the quarter."

"I went to see if there might be any fresh diggings. There were. So I went and found a digger and asked about them. He said that all the recent ones had been from *korori*." This was a word for suddenly silently dropping dead, but here it signified cholera. "I asked if there had been any with missing heads. I must be joking, he said. I asked if he saw all the corpses. Of course, he said. How else could he be sure he got them in the right holes, and that was his job. I asked how he was able to tell which was which. From photographs, mostly, he said, but he had to have help sometimes. It isn't true that foreigners all look alike, he said. Good man. Knew his business and did his duty. I didn't much like the cemetery at first. All those stones looking like ghosts about to grab you. But then I sort of got to feel at home in it. I wished I could read some of the names, but all I could read were numbers, and they didn't mean much, and names probably wouldn't have meant much either. I thought they must all be the graves of pretty girls."

"With mustaches.

"But of course there aren't many foreign women around, and I'm not sure that any at all have died."

## 5

Hanshichi was in no hurry to do anything further about the morning-glory case. He continued to feel, if vaguely, that it was no concern of his. Let samurai swells take care of their own lost heirs. Instinct, another word for experience, was bolstered by faith in the efficacy of the police system sufficient to persuade him that the Sugita boy, wherever he might be, was safe. Hanshichi and the constable had heard nothing. Therefore nothing had happened—nothing untoward, in any event.

On a lovely day in May, the most florid of months, when summer was already in the air, he took a stroll along the north bank of the Kanda River. He did not know whether he would go as far as Number Four and the Sugita house. If the impulse took him, he might. Again, he might not. Mostly he wanted the walk, which was certain to be beautiful. The river and the outer moat of the castle were among the most beautiful places in Edo, in general a handsome city, if not assertively so.

A field of purple, the embankments of the moat were indeed beautiful. It was the season for what were called flowering radishes. The flowers did look a little like radishes, but the color was richer. From a slight distance they were like violets.

Hanshichi rounded the northwest arc of the moat and was safely past the walls of the Tokugawa estate. The qualifier "safely" fitted his mood fairly well. The walls of such places were always strong, simple, and handsome. The gates and guards were another matter. They were none of these things. They were pompous. They blustered and scowled. Hanshichi hugged the embankment as closely as the path permitted, to be as far as possible from gate and guards. He did not intend to walk much farther. Soon he would have to decide whether or not to cross over and see how things were in Number Four. He did not expect to find things much different from when he had last visited. Tomorrow, or some other day, would do as well.

A man crossed a bridge some distance to the south, and came towards him.

It was Heisuke, one of the two who had been in attendance that morning on the Sugita boy.

"Good morning."

The man walked past without answering.

"Good morning. May I ask you something?"

The man turned, and continued to scowl.

Hanshichi identified himself. If the man was interested to learn the fact that he was in the presence of an officer of the law, he did not show it. He grunted.

"You are with the Sugita family, I think."

This time the man did not even grunt.

"I've heard about the family misfortune."

Probably the man would have liked to know where he had heard it. He did not say so. Hanshichi told him anyway. He told the truth, without identifying Nakajima.

"You still have no idea where the boy might be?"

"None. None at all." These monosyllables managed to get past the unrelenting scowl.

"Some say that he might have been whisked off by a fairy or something."

"Could be."

"There's not much we can do if that's the case. You can't think of anything else?"

"No."

"As I say, if fairies and such types are involved there's not much anyone can do. If not I'll find him for you, I promise I will." Hanshichi hoped to make it appear that he knew more than he was saying and more than he actually did know.

"Do you have any ideas?"

It was the longest statement the man had made. It sounded as if he would indeed like to have Hanshichi's thoughts in the matter.

"None just at the moment. But I have a great deal of experience." A little boasting sometimes served a purpose, especially with a class of people rather given to boasting. "When someone's alive he always turns up in the end."

"If you say so."

"I'm keeping you. Where are you off to?"

"Nowhere in particular. We wander around hoping we'll come on something. Do what you can."

"I mean to."

Wandering aimlessly around the city was not Hanshichi's style. He would not have said that he had been wandering aimlessly this morning. It was time he headed for home.

But he could not reverse his course immediately. Heisuke, though he proceeded on his own course, was watching him. Hanshichi went on to the next bridge, which had him very near Number Four. Heisuke continued to walk towards the walls of the grand estate, but he kept looking over his shoulder. His behavior was rather peculiar. Hanshichi expected arrogance in samurai, but in this case arrogance was mixed with furtiveness. Hanshichi thought of following him. But that would do no good. He would know that he was being followed, and one could see a great distance on a brilliant day of early summer.

So Hanshichi crossed the bridge and shortly was at Number Four. He would not have lost much even if he found nothing interesting there. There were shorter routes home than the one by which he had come. He might run into one or the other of the two women, the plain but cheerful Roku and the pretty and maybe a touch conceited Yasu. He would as soon not run into the two of them simultaneously. Each was likely to be more open when not in the presence of the other.

But this time his luck was not good. There they were coming towards him and away from the Sugita residence as he approached the latter place. Each of the women had a hamper. They were plying their trade.

"I wouldn't have found you if I'd been looking for you."

"So are you sorry you found us?" said Roku.

"Who were you looking for?" said Yasu.

"You were coming from the Sugita place?"

"I wasn't," said Roku. "I've told you I never go near the place."

"I'd say this is pretty near," said Yasu.

"I draw a line."

"And some of us don't. Which type do you like better, chief?"

Hanshichi did not know about types. But he knew which of the women he liked better and which was likely to be the more useful.

"How's business?"

Yasu shook her hamper, which was empty. Roku's did not seem to be.

"Anything new over there?" He nodded towards a corner of the Sugita property.

Yasu was the one to answer, and she did.

"Heisuke and Matazo had a big fight."

"What about?"

"Me." It was a concise answer, certainly, and a matter-of-fact one.

"You must tell me all about it. But not just at the moment. I'm in a bit of a hurry. How about this evening?"

They arranged to meet in Kanda. He hoped that Roku would have the tact not to come along. And he hoped that his wife Sen would not hear of the appointment. If she did he would say it was a business meeting. She would understand. He was sure she would understand even if the matter proceeded to the point of marital infidelity.

There must be something suspicious about him this morning. Even as Heisuke had done, the two women kept looking over their shoulders at him. They might have said that he was doing it to them. Of course he was, but only defensively. He could not see that he had an inhibiting effect on them. They did on him. Matazo was coming out the Sugita gate as he passed. He did not stop. Matazo looked grim, almost murderous. If it had not been for the women Hanshichi might have asked what the trouble was. He could have done it anyway, but he wanted Yasu to see that he was leaving Matazo under her jurisdiction. And there persisted the feeling that none of this was really his business.

A little nearer home, at the top of the hill that led down into the Kanda flatlands, he came upon some young gentlemen who were not restraining their anger. They were very young gentlemen, just at or not quite at puberty. If he had not already known it from their haircuts, he would have known from the epithets flung back and forth that they were very young samurai. They were not of the same rank. The ones most energetic with epithets and presently fists were of lower rank. Nor were the factions of equal size. The young gentlemen of lower rank greatly outnumbered those of higher rank. It was clear that the latter would have done well to turn tail and run for it. They had no chance.

It was not clear that they had much chance even of fleeing. They were surrounded. Pride of position might have persuaded them to fight on. As to that, Hanshichi had no way of knowing. What was clear was that the inferior ones were not meek about accepting their inferiority. It was class warfare, and they relished it. In addition to being more numerous, the young gentlemen of the lower order were stronger and healthier. Unless someone interfered they were certain to win, and do considerable damage to those of the higher order. Hanshichi did not propose to interfere. Let young gentlemen take care of themselves.

Attracted by the noise, the two women had come up.

"At it again," said Roku. "The ten-leggers and the eight-leggers."

Having himself grown up on the streets of Edo, Hanshichi knew that these were squids and octopuses, designations for boys involved in street brawls. The octopuses were the smaller and weaker faction, usually the one of higher rank.

"I wouldn't have been surprised to see the young master in the middle of it," said Yasu. "He generally was."

"You mean the Sugita boy?" asked Hanshichi.

"Yes.,'

"If it was anything like this one, he must have come home with a few bruises."

"Oh, someone will come along and stop it. Someone always does. I can see that you don't intend to do anything yourself. It doesn't matter. Someone will."

Someone did, an adult gentleman of the samurai class. He pushed his way into the tangle and pulled out a pale boy who obviously was not doing much for himself.

"Matazo was always rescuing the young master, may the gods preserve him."

This ended the war of fists. The war of words trailed after the two.

"We won't forget about this. We'll get even."

"They mean it. That's why the young master was always getting rescued. He wasn't a good fighter and he was always getting into fights."

This, thought Hanshichi, was interesting. He was beginning to get a sense of why the boy had disappeared.

Once more he said good-bye to the women. A kimono did not set off a female figure at all clearly, but he could tell from the rear which of the two was the more attractive. The evening might be rather good both for business and for pleasure.

He had arranged to meet Yasu at the bottom of the slope by the Kanda Shrine. He had to decide where they would go from there. It was not easy. He was well-versed in the pleasures of the great metropolis, not having spurned them back in the days before he was married, and not having completely spurned them even since. They ran several continua. One had to do with price. There were places where a laborer stopped by for a drink before dinner, and places the services of whose geisha only a merchant prince or a military one could afford. The latter sort were supposed to stay away from places frequented by townsmen, but they found ways and excuses.

Another had to do with the chastity of the personnel. The more pretentious sort of geisha called herself an artist, but the distinction between her and a whore was not always easy to make. Yet another had to do with the kind of companionship one was in quest of. To some places one could without breaching a code bring a female companion of one's own choice. At others the establishment provided women, and did not welcome them who were not on its staff or whose services it had not solicited. Edo offered almost everything in the way of carnal and gustatory pleasure, but the variety sometimes made things difficult. It was so easy to misjudge, and, with the best intentions, end up by insulting someone.

He finally selected a place that lay midway along several continua, and a place where a decision as to how to spend the night could be postponed. A man could wait and see how things went, and at in-between places a dining chamber could easily be converted to a sleeping chamber.

He told Sen that he would be out late. Indeed business might keep him out all night. She was not to sit up and she was not to worry. If she had suspicions she did not let them show.

The lateness of the hour deprived him of choices that would have been available earlier. Darkness came late these long spring evenings. He did not want to be with her in broad daylight. Most people in Kanda knew who she was and what trade she plied. The restaurant would be discommoded if they came for dinner at eight or so and did not stay the night. Word would spread, and his reputation would be damaged, and success in his business depended in considerable measure on reputation, Well, it could not be helped. He must hope that all went well, not that he was exactly sure what he meant by the expression.

In fact events proceeded as well as he could have hoped. Dinner was good but not excessively so. It would be hard for a meal to be excessively delicious, but a Japanese meal could be excessively pretty. He pressed sake on her. She turned very red but went on drinking. As the fruit course came she passed out, quietly and without ostentation. The waitresses were untroubled. They cleared away the dishes and laid out bedding where the table had been. The two had earlier changed to cotton kimonos and been to the bath. These little rites were standard. One was obliged to go through them even if one did not much want to. Hanshichi was in the small minority that found one bath a day quite enough. Firm young flesh and smooth young skin did beguile the tedium, however.

As soon as the maids had departed she was ready to go. Unless he asked he could not be sure whether the lapse into unconsciousness had been an act. He might not even then, and he did not ask. She lay down with her arms, though not her legs quite yet, spread wide.

They got on well. In the uninhibited talk that adds so much to the aftermath of such an engagement, she likened him to a stud-horse and he likened her to an octopus trap.

As they were warming up for a second one he asked a few questions. Wooden clappers passed in the street below, a sort of curfew, warning that fires could be dangerous. Otherwise, save for the distant barking of a dog, the city was silent. It went to bed early and got up early.

"So Matazo and Heisuke had a fight."

"So that's why you brought me here."

"I brought you here because I wanted to."

"You can tell me the truth. It won't bother me. And maybe you don't know what it means for someone like me to be in a place like this with someone like you. Don't be surprised if I start asking favors. Oh. All ready for another go. It would seem."

"You aren't exactly frigid yourself. But it will be better if we wait a little."

"Better how?"

"Like this." He probed silently for a time.

"What was the fight about?"

"I've already told you. Me."

"That doesn't tell me very much."

"Matazo promised me some money. But he doesn't have any."

"What for?"

"What business is that of yours?"

"Would you rather I asked how much money?"

"That's no answer."

"It's all grist." He said literally that he was the sort of person who never stumbled without picking something up.

"He promised me something for the hot weather. A girl can't go around all sweaty and smelly."

"It's not very good for a boy either."

"It's very good for a stud-horse. Gathers them like flies."

"That's a valuable piece of information."

"Your grist for the evening. You don't need to ask any more questions."

"Why did he go to Heisuke?"

"Well, for one thing, Heisuke has money. He holds on to it."

"He's not the only man in the world that does."

"Do you?"

"It doesn't matter. He'd never come to me."

"You're too far above him."

"The opposite. Daimyo may go to rich dealers for big money, but ordinary samurai don't come to people like me for chicken feed."

"It takes more than chicken feed to get me the kind of summer wardrobe I'm accustomed to."

"All right, stud-horse feed. My question is still the same. Why did he go to Heisuke?"

"He seems to think Heisuke owes it to him. And I know what your next question is. Why? You should know my answer. I haven't the faintest notion."

"And you don't want to know?"

"Why should I?"

"As a favor to me. It could have a lot to do with the Sugita boy that disappeared."

"In contrast to all the Sugita boys that didn't disappear? There's only one."

"That's a quibble."

"It's such fun to quibble with cops and constables. But if I can do a favor for a man that does so much for me, fine. What shall I do?"

"Keep your eyes, ears, etc., open."

"Easy enough. And how do I let you know if something comes up?"

This did present difficulties. He did not want to tell her the honest truth, that he had already learned as much from her as he hoped to learn.

"Well, there's that bond we remarked on. We keep running into each other. And you can come running or send someone else running if something comes up."

"Running where? You're never at home."

"You're sure of that? Anyhow Sen always knows where to find me."

"Even tonight."

"You're not to think that this is my usual sort of night. Anyhow. Nothing in this world is certain. I think I've heard the old man up the back alley say so. We'll have to trust to luck. I'm a pretty lucky sort."

"You do seem to get what you want."

"True. Very true."

He laid an exploring hand on her, and they were at it again.

He was afraid he looked a little haggard when he got home the next morning. Sen asked no questions.

The truth about the troubles at morning-glory house was not far away, he thought. He thought he knew who the immediate culprits were. What exactly they had done and who exactly was behind it would emerge presently. They had not acted on their own. The risk was high, and they were not stupid. Heads rolled and bellies got ripped open for less. And it was clear from what Yasu had told him that a considerable amount of money was involved.

He sent for Matsu, who had not come around in quite some time. He practically lived over east of the river these days, said the old woman from whom Matsu, a bachelor, rented a room.

When, the next day, Matsu did come around, it turned out that he had been not over east of the river but down in Yokohama. The pursuit of all the Saburos in all the temple archives east of the river was taking too much time and had long since become tedious. No word had come for some days from Goro.

Goro's explanation for his silence was brief and convincing. He had nothing to report. Or at any rate he had had nothing until yesterday or so. Now something had come up. He would shortly have sent a message off to Matsu if Matsu himself had not appeared. There was evidence that Lloyd, the Englishman, was preparing to depart. The magistracy did not know when he would be departing.

It was information which the foreign companies did not have to report, and they did not report anything voluntarily, except of course when they were victims of Japanese molestation.

"If he goes we probably will never know the truth."

"Would it matter? Good riddance is what I say."

"Maybe it wouldn't matter to you. But I've put in a lot of time into it. And what about all the points you said I would make? And what about all the points you yourself wanted to make with all the pawnbrokers?"

"Good. We like our youngsters to be upright and outspoken."

"I suppose you'll tell me next that you said it to make me that way."

"Good, good. More outspoken all the time. But what brings you back to Edo when you face a big crisis down in Yokohama?"

"We've done what we could down there, and we've made it easier to get something done here in Edo. I spent the night down there and yes I spent it exactly where you think I spent it, and came back up to Edo yesterday."

So they had spent night before last in a similar fashion. Which told of one of those bonds.

"You'll be very proud of me," said Matsu, when Hanshichi did not ask what they had done. It would have been good if he had shown an amount of interest, but a person could not have everything.

"Of course," said Hanshichi. "If you think I would have expected anything less you underrate both of us. Tell me."

"We had a talk with Lloyd."

"Well, now. I am proud of you. You and Goro? And you were afraid to go into Dr. Hepburn's office."

"It wasn't easy."

"I'm sure it wasn't at all easy. I'm very proud of you. How did you manage?"

"Goro knows a little English and Lloyd knows a little Japanese. We managed. Probably better than with an interpreter. I suspect the magistrate's office doesn't use interpreters because it doesn't have any good ones. They say they're better at Dutch, but who knows? There are hardly any Dutchmen around."

"How do you know they're no good?"

"I've spent quite a few hours at the magistrate's office. They don't make any sense. Don't you think that's a pretty good indication?"

"Unless maybe they're translating English or something that doesn't make any. But I'm not arguing with you. Go on."

"He wouldn't tell us anything about himself. Seems to have some funny foreign notion that he has a right not to say anything about himself. There's not much we can do about it. I wonder how it is with the consulate. We didn't find out if he's leaving and if so why and when. He wouldn't even tell us what he and Saburo were fighting about that night."

"That leaves only Saburo. I suppose he did tell you something about Saburo."

"He didn't tell us anything about his dealings with Saburo. But he'd be pleased if we put Saburo in jail. We could tell that by the tone of his voice."

"Did he tell you anything that will keep you from ruining your eyes over temple scribblings?"

"Something that might. He said that Saburo lives near a bridge."

"Edo may not have many big bridges but it has hundreds of little ones."

"He said it was a big bridge across the big river."

"He called it the big river?"

"Yes. Just like an Edo man."

For sons of Edo "the big river" was the Sumida. They had ways of distinguishing between "the big river" and "a big river" in spite of the fact that the Japanese language contained no articles.

"The bridges across the big river can keep you busy for a while. Did he know which one?"

"No. But he had something as good as a name. He and Saburo came up to Edo and watched fireworks one night last summer and then went to Saburo's place."

"Ryogoku, of course. So you move from one sinful place to another."

"Get moved, would be more like it."

"Well, don't get the clap. And watch your wallet."

These few words would have given a stranger to Edo a good idea of what Ryogoku was like. The two approaches to Ryogoku Bridge were among the most bustling parts of the city, and they bustled with dubious people and attractions. They had a big temple and a red-light district, and these two elements were important for any Edo place that wished to bustle, and they offered little besides debauchery. One might go to the bustle of Asakusa or Shitaya to view cherry blossoms, but not to that of Ryogoku.

"And are you putting all your eggs in one basket after all?"

"Trouble is I only have one just at the moment. If what I want isn't there I don't know where else to look."

"That's the wrong spirit. What about the monkey man and the butterfly man?"

"But they were Americans."

"You've acquired too much knowledge of the world for me. Explain yourself."

"It's not that I know so much. But I know people who know a lot and are willing to share what they know."

"That's what keeps the country going. I suppose Goro is one of them?"

"Goro is a good fellow, but he hasn't been around very long. I meant people who've been around ever since the first red beard showed up."

"You were saying?"

"Remind me."

"Something about Americans."

"It's not always easy to know what kind of European you're up against when it is a European. Or so I'm told. There are more English around than anyone else. So you're chances are good when you assume it's an Englishman."

"When in doubt say English. And the Americans?"

"They're a pretty stupid lot and they let themselves get used. I've found out a little more about gold rushes. You have to be pretty stupid to let yourself get caught up in one. Maybe you have to be stupid to let yourself get caught up in America in the first place."

And maybe we're lucky Lord Somebody and Lord Somebody Else took all the gold before we could get near it. Whoever is involved in this case isn't being used. They're in it together. You'll understand, I'm sure, why I may have to take a few more walks down to Yokohama."

"Oh but of course. Ryogoku has no class. I've been meaning to ask: do they have any red-headed blue-eyed and so on whores down in Yokohama?"

Matsu tried to look offended, but looked sheepish instead.

"Of course not," he said. "Would you include Chinese?" he added.

"Of course not. When will you be going back down to Yokohama?"

"Why? Do you want to go along?"

"That didn't sound very friendly."

"I'd love to have you along. Did that? Except maybe on a Sunday."

"When is Sunday?"

For the Edo townsman every day was like every other day, except for a very few holidays, no more than two or three a year, excluding funerals.

"Day after tomorrow, and every seventh day afterwards."

"I hope you don't expect me to remember that."

"You asked. And I think maybe you'd better start remembering. Sunday is important to them, and it will be to us too, when we get in the swing of things. We'll all go to church and then we'll all go out for a horseback ride."

"Anything wrong with that?"

"The church part is boring and the horseback part asks for trouble."

"Trouble is the name of our business."

"But we don't go out asking for it. So I was taught by my revered master, anyhow."

"I never taught you to run away from it."

"But it's so complicated when it involves foreigners. I go the other way whenever I see a horse with red hair on it. Street wisdom it's called down in Yokohama."

"I think maybe you've seen about enough of Yokohama."

"I hope you're not saying I should throw the case over."

"Of course not. But I sometimes find myself with a case on my hands I wish I'd never heard of. I happen to have one now."

"The morning-glory one. I wouldn't want it either."

As if suspecting that Hanshichi might not be above foisting it on him, Matsu started off in an easterly direction, no doubt to hunt for Saburos.

"How will you know when you have the right one?" Hanshichi called after him.

"The right one?"

"The right Saburo. There must be dozens of Saburos within shouting distance of Ryogoku Bridge. Hundreds."

"Thousands, I'm sure. You don't remember what he looked like?"

"Just the hairdo."

"That's enough. There can't be many hairdos like that in Ryogoku. It's a conservative place."

The Saburo they had seen in the Yokohama had patronized a foreign-style barber, probably a Japanese one. Stiff spikes of hair shooting off at random. It was an instance of new techniques facing stubborn traditional resistance. The same was true of the man's dress, though he wore Western dress more comfortably than most Japanese. Western dress could be more readily accommodated to Ryogoku than the hairdo, unless it was a wig.

"What are you smirking about?" He did not immediately recognize the voice. Maybe this was because it was farther away than he was accustomed to having it. Yasu was the possessor.

"Thank you for the other night," he said, having assured himself that Roku was not within earshot.

"Oh, the pleasure was all mine," she replied, her hands over her cheeks as if to conceal a blush.

"And why aren't you about your business?"

"Now which business would that be I wonder."

"These aren't exactly business hours for the one I don't

mean." He lifted her basket. "You haven't sold a thing. If you don't do it now when are you going to?"

"Oh, it'll be empty in no time once I get started. I'm not like Roku. I have good generous dependable customers."

"Not in this neighborhood."

"I'm thinking of starting another business in this neighborhood. An information network, with a very limited clientele. Maybe when I tell you what happened last night you'll want to come over tonight."

"I'm a happily married man. I can't go spending every night away from home."

"And did you spend last night away from home?"

"You can find the answer to that one with a little imagination."

But just then Sen came in the door. She had been out to buying onions. At any rate they were what showed. Proud purple onions. The two women greeted each other cordially. If Sen suspected anything she did not show it.

"So when and where tonight? You haven't told me what happened last night."

"I saw the two of them by the moat. Heisuke and Matazo. They were having an argument." Sen had seemed mildly interested until she heard the two masculine names. "I wasn't close enough to hear what the argument was about, but I can guess. Me." Sen was interested once more. "I pulled back into an alley when they started coming my way. I didn't catch much that they said. If I'd caught any less I wouldn't have caught anything at all. 'Tomorrow,' Matazo said."

"Meaning?"

"You're the only detective around. Unless Sen is one too."

"The detective's wife is not a happy one," said Sen. Only I think maybe I'd be more inclined to say flatfoot's."

"When was it?"

"Oh along towards the beginning of the Hour of the Chicken, I'd say."

"You might be a little more precise."

"I wouldn't remember that much except it's my favorite hour. Shall I meet you and show you the spot?"

"How do you know it will be the same spot?"

"I've told you everything I know. I thought you might be interested."

"Along towards early in the Hour of the Chicken, then. I like it too. Isn't that nice." The Hour of the Chicken stretched, these long spring days, from evening into night. Indeed it was a pleasant time, especially for the masculine half of Edo, which drank it away.

"Where?"

Hanshichi suggested the drinking place where he had encountered Roku. Yasu did not think that a good idea. Matazo would need reinforcement. The place in question would be the most convenient of places for obtaining it. Hanshichi did not ask why reinforcement would be necessary. Matazo was not, it seemed, a valiant sort, and valor would be appropriate.

So they agreed to meet at a corner of a mansion they both knew. It had a dry moat. Many aristocratic mansions in that part of the city did. The chief purpose of a moat in these peaceful days, though they were not as peaceful as they had once been, was display. Keeping water in a moat high upon a hill, and it was a hilly part of the city, could be bothersome.

"Jump in if anyone challenges you. Actually it's a walk-in moat that invites more people than it turns away. I've had good times down there."

A trouble with "early in the evening" was that it was not at all precise. Edo was not well provided with time pieces. Hanshichi had bought a watch down in Yokohama, but he was sure that Yasu had none. If she had one she would not be hiding it from the world.

As he approached the dry moat his watch told him that the Hour of the Chicken had come.

A slight distance beyond the dry moat, which encircled only the one mansion, someone was waiting. Most likely it was Matazo. Heisuke would come up grandly and tardily. Fortunately the man was looking the other way. Hanshichi took Yasu's advice and dived into the moat.

"Imagine meeting you here." She was there ahead of him, obviously for the same reason. "It's a shame we don't have time for a good time."

"And did you have a good day?"

"Depends. My basket was empty in no time, which made it a good day, I suppose, sort of, but not much better than most of them. Nothing else happened. which made it not such a good day."

"That was Matazo up there?"

"Of course. My idea was that we'd get here first and hide in the big moat, and find a good place to stand and listen. We can still do it if we're lucky. This is too far away."

"The big moat" was the outer castle moat, across the street from this more private moat. There was little danger of detection where they were. The dead weeds from the preceding year were shoulder high and even higher.

" Let's make sure exactly where he is, and while we're about it make sure that no one else is coming along." She raised her head over the rim of the moat. "Just above where the night heron always is. I hope it's there tonight."

"I hope it isn't. I don't like night herons. And they don't like me."

"Let's hope it doesn't recognize you."

She led him to a segment of the moat from which Matazo was not visible. Then they hurried past a few dark buildings, and Edo was a very dark city even at the Hour of the Chicken, and came out on "the big moat." She pushed him over and jumped over herself. The embankment was steep, and the weeds from the year before had been cut back. There was nothing to hold to. He rolled and slid most of the way to the water.

"Do you have to make so much noise?" She had come quietly down the embankment behind him.

"I would welcome recommendations as to how to avoid it. In the circumstances. I suppose it was you that pushed me?"

"Heisuke was coming. Didn't you see him?"

He had to confess that he did not. She said that he was not a very good excuse for a detective.

"If you wish. Anyhow, neither of them saw us. It's because we're both dressed in black. Like a pair of peepers."

"I can't see either of them up there."

"The best possible evidence that neither of them saw us."

"Where are you, night heron? It's not easy to spot a night heron at night."

"It dresses like a peeper, and it's-a better peeper than we will ever be."

"Ah, there you are, right at your post, faithful creature."

"The picture of greed and gluttony."

And indeed it was a sinister creature, low and squat for a heron, not black like Hanshichi and Oyasu but a murky gray. Though without question aware of their presence, it was motionless, its great scimitar of a beak pointed at the water, waiting for a fish to come swimming up. One did, just as they were passing. The beak darted forward. The fish was a large one, too large to swallow, Hanshichi would have thought. The heron did not agree. It shook the fish from side to side as a dog might shake a rabbit. When the threshing had subsided, the heron gulped and the fish went down. Then the heron resumed its position, waiting for another fish.

"See what I mean? That was enough to keep it for a week."

There came a horrible scream. Heisuke's head and shoulders emerged above the rim of the moat. He did not see them.

"That was good of it. Now we know exactly where he is."

"It doesn't like me."

"I doubt that it much likes anyone. And it did us a good turn."

They climbed, hugging close to the embankment, lest either of the men chanced to look over.

Presently they heard voices. When they had climbed far enough to understand what was being said, Matazo was speaking.

"It's not enough," he was saying. "You can do better than that. For an old friend."

"A man can only do what he can do. What about the money I gave you last time?"

"I lost it playing with the boys in the fire station."

"You have to stop gambling. All it means is getting peeled away layer by layer."

"Of course it does. I don't excuse myself. But you know what I promised her." Yasu nudged Hanshichi and pointed at herself. "She keeps after me. I'm a man, and I have to keep my promises. And you have to help me."

"I'm not sure you are a man. A man would just give her what he promised her."

"But you have to help me."

"Yes, old friend. Do you think I have a steady income? Do you think I have enough stored up to look after someone else? I pick up what I can where I can."

"I'm not asking you for money. I'm asking you to ask her."

"Ask Yasu for money for whatever you promised her?"

"You know who I mean. There's only person I could mean."

"Mrs. Sugita. You're saying I can keep going to her for money? I gave you half of what I got, and I can't expect more. And you have nothing to complain about."

"I'm not saying I have. I'm just asking you to help me out." Matazo took on a wheedling tone. "You have to. She's pestering me to death. You know how it is. You've had the same experience. You should be able to sympathize, just a little."

Heisuke did not answer. Matazo's tone now turned threatening.

"You won't help me. All right. There's one thing more I can do. Mr. Nakajima was at the constable's office this morning. And any fool can guess why he was there. Maybe I'll pay a little visit myself."

"You've been to too many bad plays." Heisuke laughed scornfully. "Go try it on someone else. I'm not the man for you."

Now they were shouting at each other. Unable to win the argument, Matazo had a try at physical combat. Heisuke was the better trained in the martial arts. Soon Matazo was flat on the dusty path.

"We're drifters, you and I. Where do you suggest we drift off to if we get kicked out of this place?"

Hanshichi pulled himself over the rim of the moat. Heisuke was walking away. Matazo was dusting himself off.

"Good evening," said Hanshichi. "I think you need a drink."

Matazo recognized Hanshichi in the moonlight, for the moon was just coming over the trees, and seemed to agree. Yasu had gone down to join the night heron. Hanshichi now had a clear theory about the case of Morning-glory House. He would go around tomorrow and present it to the constable, who would have no trouble testing it. He certainly hoped very much that it proved correct. He wanted to be rid of the case. He wanted samurai to stay in their place and he would stay in his. Besides, Yasu was too close a neighbor for comfort.

In his cups, Matazo obliquely and unconsciously confirmed the theory.

# 6

Hanshichi did not go to the constable's office until the next afternoon. Timing was important. If he went early in the morning it might seem that he had stayed awake all night in his eagerness, which in turn would suggest supreme confidence. He could not be sure that his theory was right. So he did not want to put too fine a point on it and be hugely mortified if it was wrong. By going in the afternoon he could make it seem that he had other business over by the river, the case of the spooky dance teacher, perhaps, and had dropped by with an idea that had slipped into his mind somewhere along the way.

"About the Sugita boy," said Hanshichi, when he and the constable had exchanged pleasantries about the weather (spring was at its best), the spooky teacher (she had probably been murdered, but they were professionals who knew how not to be horrified), and similar subjects.

"Wish we'd never heard of him."

"Just what I was saying to my wife." A way of avoiding full responsibility suddenly came to him. A professional avoided full responsibility when possible. "She thinks you should have someone search the rooms of the two men who were with the boy the morning he disappeared."

"You discuss these things with your wife?"

"Oh, sometimes I feel a little out of my depth and look for an outside opinion. I hope I will not seem forward in asking whether the same might not be true in your own exalted case."

The constable was suitably amused, and let the matter pass. "And why does your good wife make the suggestion?"

"She thinks we're more likely to come on something in Matazo's room." This was, of course, what Hanshichi himself thought.

"Matazo and Heisuke are the two men, I'm sure you remember. Matazo eats too much, especially for someone who spends a good deal more time drinking than eating. My wife knows this for a fact. She got it from a woman who takes meals to the bachelors in the compound. I happen to know for a fact myself (overheard it by the moat one night) that the two of them are fighting over money. The money they're fighting over came from Mrs. Sugita. Sen is sure it has something to do with the morning-glory thing. The curse. You remember that, I'm sure. They found a morning glory somewhere on the grounds during the summer, and the curse was sure to strike again. Of course not everyone thought so. It's the sort of thing a woman would worry about, Sen says. She'd make a good police woman. Do you think we'll ever have police women?"

"I wouldn't be surprised at anything, now that we've let the barbarians in. Do you want to do the searching yourself? I can give you credentials."

"I'd rather not. I haven't liked anything about the case." This was not quite true. He had enjoyed the Yasu episodes, though he would as soon put them behind him, along with the rest of the case.

"You prefer murders?"

"As long as the parties concerned are my sort. The people over there aren't."

"I'll have someone take a look."

"He's welcome to all the credit if he wants. I just want to be finished with it."

But in fact Hanshichi received due credit. He learned later in the day that the boy had been found in Matazo's closet.

Yet a bit later he heard that Matazo had run off. He was, as Heisuke had said, a drifter, with no firm place on the Sugita table of organization. It took a while, because of her loose habits, to establish that Yasu too had disappeared. The conclusion seemed unavoidable that she had actually been fond of him, and that the two had run off together. Hanshichi would not have thought it possible. Even the best detective is sometimes misled. He would not have liked to admit that he was relieved. He would have tired of her. Sen was a more interesting woman, basically, and Yasu could have become an embarrassment.

It came to seem that Heisuke meant to blast his way through. Something of the sort was also necessary for Mrs. Sugita. It was clear to almost everyone that, terrified of the morning-glory curse and the possibility that her only child would be waylaid on his way to the examination that dark morning, she had paid the two men to bring him back to the Sugita mansion. There he had been ever since. Mrs. Sugita would not have found it easy to explain the truth to her husband. She and Heisuke tried to tell people that the boy had been spirited off. He had been taken away, no one knew where, how, or why, and had come back in a similarly mysterious fashion.

But Mr. Sugita was no fool, and the boy was intelligent, if not the best fighter in the neighborhood. He saw only trouble ahead of he tried to conceal the truth from his father. He had no good reason for doing so, except possibly to protect his mother, and the samurai code placed loyalty and obedience to father and master (the two were often the same) above most virtues. Asked why he had not gone to his father earlier, he replied, and it was a good point, that he had been as good as imprisoned.

People felt a little sorry for Matazo. It came out that he had been deceived. Heisuke had taken for himself more than half the amount received from Mrs. Sugita, and divided only the remainder with Matazo. Matazo and Yasu were not heard from further in Kanda or Number Four.

Some felt sorry for Mrs. Sugita as well, although even they who did thought her a proper fool, and what can anyone do with or for a proper fool? She was sent back to the family seat in the provinces. Effectively divorced, she lived with her own family and not his. People sighed and said that her motives had been good.

Heisuke's punishment was the harshest. If anyone sympathized no one said so. As was his prerogative, Mr. Sugita ordered him to disembowel himself. Mr. Sugita could merely have lopped his head off, and that too would have been his prerogative. Disembowelment was in theory voluntary, and was considered a fitting conclusion to a warrior's life. So in a sense, given the times and their morals, Mr. Sugita acted magnanimously. Heisuke was a craven wretch, but he did cling to the bottom reaches of the warrior class, and was permitted to die as a warrior.

"It just goes to show you," said Matsu, who came by one day and acquired all this information

He was still commuting between Edo and Yokohama. Hanshichi thought that he was spending too much time on the case of the severed head. A good policeman (policeman, detective, very much the same thing under the system) had a sense for these things. Matsu was young and inexperienced, and had not yet arrived at one. A good policeman made a mental reckoning as soon as he took a case. It told him how much time the case was worth. Hanshichi had taken a chance in the morning-glory case. He had not been as sure of the solution as he pretended to be, but he had spent enough time on it.

He waited for Matsu to continue. "I'm sure it does," he said, and waited some more.

"You can't avoid fate," said Matsu finally. Apparently in a contemplative mood, he fell silent again.

"I'm sure that's so," said Hanshichi after a time. "But here we have what some people think is a curse and some people don't."

"Same thing. You can't avoid fate, you can't avoid a curse. Same thing. She thought she could protect the boy from the curse: And it turned on her. It was going to get someone. When she tried to turn it away from the boy it got her."

This seemed very wise for so young a man.

Neither of them mentioned Heisuke, the most grievously injured (unless Matsuzo was out starving to death somewhere, which did not seem likely, since he seemed to have Yasu, who could always make a living for them). Maybe it was because he had done what he did for money, and so was not as clear an object lesson. Maybe it was because what happened to him could have happened to almost any man in Edo.

"You never can tell. Now tell me about your own business."

"I think I'll be back in Edo for a while."

"Tired of Yokohama?"

"Well, Edo is a lot bigger, and it's home. But that's not the point. Neither of them is the point. I can't do much about Lloyd. So I have to find Saburo. Or drop the case, after all the time I've put into it."

"What I generally do when there's only one lead and it looks like a pretty good one is I have a go at bullying."

"I couldn't even if I could."

This was somewhat enigmatic. Hanshichi waited. "I can't lay a hand on a foreigner. You know that. Don't tell me we'll get rid of them all some day. You don't know that even if you say so, and it hasn't happened yet. And if we are to get rid of them we can't go in for bullying. We can trick them, maybe, but not bully them."

"So maybe I should get out of this business and enjoy my last years." Hanshichi was only forty, but a man was held in those days to have nothing to complain about if he died at fifty. "Tell me about this new day. I face a decision."

His tone was bantering, but Matsu did tell him.

"If we're to get rid of the foreign courts we keep complaining about we have to make them think we're just like them. Or just like what they say they are. I'm not sure it's the truth, but they say they never bully a suspect. They may trick him and bribe him, but they don't bully him. They're supposed to find good solid evidence against him. I wonder if they always do. Anyway, it's what they say they do, and what we have to do."

"Makes me feel sorry for young fellows like you."

"I sort of feel sorry for myself. Goro was right about the Thompson business. They could make a suit and probably a fairly good one if someone wanted it, but mostly they change money. Saburo has to be in Edo. Lloyd is getting ready to leave. I wish I knew why. Goro is keeping an eye on him. There's not much more he can do."

"But there are other things you could do with Saburo. If you're dying to be a man of the new day maybe we won't be able to work together much longer. We won't argue about it. Maybe some time, but not now."

"It doesn't seem right that I should be lecturing you. But have you already forgotten what we learned from the morning-glory case?"

"It's easy to forget what you don't really believe in the first place. Which should answer your penetrating question. It doesn't seem anything but right that I should be lecturing you, and I say you're taking too much time on the Yokohama case."

"Maybe. But the more time you put into a case the more you lose by ditching it."

"That's hard to deny."

Matsu was suddenly eager. "Is there something I should be working on instead? I'm beginning to think after all—"

Hanshichi waited.

"Edo is more interesting than Yokohama."

"At least the new day will be slower in coming. You remember the case of the dance teacher."

"The spooky dance teacher? Of course. I was there the morning you heard about it."

It had been on a festival morning not long before. There was scarcely a day the whole year through when some shrine or temple was not having a festival. So the industrious citizenry could scarcely take a holiday for each one. Pillars of the community, however, generally made token observance of the larger and more famous ones. Hanshichi had gone before dawn to pay his respects to the Kannon of Asakusa, in the biggest temple all up and down the Sumida. He arrived before even the pigeons were stirring. There was only a scattering of worshipers. So he had ample time for what he most wanted to do, attract the attention of the goddess herself. There was already a summer heaviness and rancidity in the air.

Having had his leisurely audience with the goddess, he started back towards Kanda. It was not yet full daylight. The day promised to be a warm one. Late spring could be warmer than early summer, which was often filled with rain.

He approached the Shogun's Road, which ran north and south just east of Kanda, and took its popular name from the fact that the shogun used it for visits to the graves of earlier shoguns, on the grounds of a large temple in Ueno. A cluster of men was standing at the entrance to an alley. He recognized several of them, including Matsu. He had not known that Matsu was in Edo, but was not surprised that he should be, given the nature of the case on which he was at work, that of the severed alien head.

A man from the lower ranks of the police organization seemed to be in command of whatever the occasion was. Him too Hanshichi recognized.

"The spooky dance teacher," he said.

Hanshichi knew who was meant. Everyone in this part of Edo knew about the spooky dance teacher. Licensed in one of the schools of Edo dance, she had adopted a young woman as her heir. The latter was pretty and in delicate health. Because of the former attribute, there was a sudden increase in the number of young men coming for lessons. The older teacher hoped to attract larger game. In this she was successful. A man of importance on the staff of a daimyo made overtures. He wished to have the younger woman as a mistress. He offered sums of money sufficient to keep the older woman in comfort. The younger woman would of course be kept in a different fashion.

It was a stroke of great good fortune for both of them. The older woman was ready to affix her seal to the contract immediately. Unfortunately the younger woman demurred. Given her precarious health, she said, she would much prefer to go on as she was. She was not up to bold demarches. The older woman ranted and stormed and wept and gnashed her teeth, but to no avail. The opportunity of a lifetime and more slipped by. Although no formal rejection of his offer was sent, nothing more was heard from the suitor, if such he may be called. The younger woman said she would do everything she was capable of to make amends.

This monstrous misfortune turned the older woman into a tyrant. She knew very well that it was her daughter and not she who brought in pupils. So, making cynical use of the promise, she had the daughter in the studio giving lessons all the day through. She had scarcely time to eat and not much time to sleep. She took to her bed. Relentless, the older woman had her up again and back in the studio. For some weeks she languished, and then she died. She collapsed in the studio, in the middle of a dancing lesson.

Rumors began to spread. The Festival of the Dead came in late summer. Newly departed spirits were especial objects of attention, and of course the young teacher was among them. The housemaid who worked for the two teachers swore that on the first night of the festival she saw the ghost of the young teacher. In a chilly breeze that came from nowhere, in the dim candlelight of the festival lantern, she saw the young woman, looking as if she could not decide where she might be. Trembling with fear, the maid told the story to people she knew.

The older woman was not popular in the neighborhood. The story accumulated new details. Faintly, deep in the night, it was said, there would be sounds in the studio as of dancing feet. There were the sounds, but there was no dancer. It came to be accepted knowledge that the teacher's house was haunted, and so everyone began calling her the spooky dance teacher. Fewer and fewer young men came asking for lessons. Since they had been attracted by the younger teacher, most of them would probably have stopped coming anyway, but the now generally accepted fact that the studio was haunted also had something to do with the matter. The murder of the older woman occurred on the anniversary of the death of the younger.

"How did it happen?" Hanshichi asked Matsu. "Did she eat something bad? She was a kind that would eat anything."

Although he had had some experience of murders, Matsu was clearly shaken.

"She was strangled by a snake."

"Oh? Then it wasn't really a murder."

Matsu did not seem to hear.

"The maid found her in the mosquito net this morning. A black snake was coiled around her neck. So she had her revenge. The young teacher, I mean. Never let a woman die on you when she has a grudge against you."

"A valuable piece of advice."

Clearly Matsu thought that the younger woman, the foster daughter, had assumed the shape of a snake—it was a thing which women who died unhappy were much given to doing—and strangled her mother. The other people, mostly men, for women tended to explore such incidents beside communal wells and over laundry tubs, seemed to agree. The fear in their eyes spoke of a brush with a ghost.

Hanshichi had doubts.

"Let's go have a look."

The crowd was thicker as they proceeded up the alley.

"And on the anniversary," someone said.

"Horrible. But I was sure something like this would happen."

Hanshichi went into the house through the back door. It was dark. The shutters had not been opened. The mosquito net had not been taken down. In a small room-off the dance teacher's bedroom the maid and the landlord, the owner of the dancing teacher's house, were sitting silently, as if afraid to breath. Hanshichi recognized the landlord.

"A terrible thing," he said.

"It certainly will do no good"

Not unnaturally, the landlord was preoccupied with his own affairs. It would be difficult if not impossible to rent the house. But then, thought Hanshichi, houses in this part of town seldom lasted more than a couple of decades. Tear it down, put it back up again and even the women by the wells would stop talking.

"You've reported it, of course."

"Yes. I can't do anything till someone from the constable's office has a look."

"Do you often see snakes hereabouts?"

"You know how crowded these parts are, one house jammed in against another. You rarely come on a snake or a frog or a toad. And it doesn't have much of a garden, maybe ten by three or four. There wouldn't be room for a snake. And it's hard to imagine how a snake could have found its way in. And there have been more rumors about the place than there is any good reason for."

Tear it down the minute you get the corpse off your hands, Hanshichi wanted to say. You can afford it. Instead he said: "May I have a look?"

"Please, please." Even as Hanshichi recognized the landlord, the landlord recognized Hanshichi.

Hanshichi went into the next room, slightly larger than the one he had just been in. At one corner was an alcove in which hung a religious painting that had not been well tended to. He would not have been surprised if it had shed a few fragments in the brief moment that it had his attention. A mosquito net almost filled the room. The weather had been warm these past few days.

The corpse lay on summer matting. The hair was somewhat disordered.

A light coverlet had been pushed to the legs. The hair was somewhat disorderd. It lay diagonally across the matting, from which the head protruded. The pillow had been shoved to one side. There was a frown on the face, the lips were twisted, a whitish tongue showed itself. The nightdress was open from kimono to sash, revealing a bosom so flat that it might have been a man's.

"Where's the snake?" asked the landlord, who had followed him into the room.

"It's too dark," said Hanshichi, who had lifted an edge of the mosquito net and gone inside. "Open one of the shutters, if you will, please."

The landlord did. Early-morning light from the garden streamed in. It turned the new mosquito net white. The face of the dancing teacher was almost as white, and rather horrible. A scaly creature shone dully and darkly below the white jaw. The landlord, still outside the mosquito net, involuntarily pulled back.

Hanshichi had a closer look. The only surprising detail was that the snake was not a large one, no more than a foot long. The tail was loosely coiled around the woman's neck. The flattish head was on the bedding. Wondering whether it was alive, Hanshichi flipped a finger against the head. It moved. He now pressed down on it with paper which he took from the breast of his kimono. As if frightened, the snake pulled its head in. Then, without resistance, the head fell again to the bedding.

Hanshichi rinsed his hands in a basin at the veranda and went again to the smaller room.

"Have you figured it out?" asked the landlord.

"I can't say anything till the constable's office has a look. Whoever they send is sure to have ideas. I'll be back later."

The landlord had hoped for something more conclusive.

"The maid," said Hanshichi. "She seems very young."

"Sixteen, I believe. You surely don't think she did it?"

"I can't say. Keep your eyes open. Being sixteen doesn't mean she had nothing to do with it."

Matsu followed him out.

"What do you make of it?" he asked.

"I can tell you what I couldn't tell him. She wasn't killed by the snake. A human being killed her and wrapped the snake around he neck afterwards. I'm sure of it."

"So it wasn't a ghost that had a grudge?" Matsu seemed doubtful and a touch disappointed.

"A ghost with a grudge may have something to do with it, but a living person with a grudge is more to the point. Did she have money?"

"She had a reputation for stinginess. Probably she put together quite a heap."

"Did she have a boy friend?

Matsu laughed. "You had a good look at her. What do you think? Besides, she wasn't interested in anything but money."

"Well, I'll be off chasing after a hunch or two. How are things down in Yokohama?"

"Oh, about the same. I was coming to see you. Another pawnbroker's been hit. And Lloyd will be going home in a few days. The Englishman that liked the whore, down in Yokohama."

"Well, if there's been a new pawnbroker, I suppose you could say we have a new case. I hadn't heard of it."

"Way out east beyond the river. Out at the edge of town. I probably wouldn't have heard of it myself if I hadn't been spending so much time in Ryogoku. Interesting place. How about a tour? There aren't many places I know more about than you do."

"One of my hunches is maybe I'll need one. My advice to you is drop the Yokohama thing and come back to Tokyo."

"I don't intend to drop the case for a while, but I am dropping Yokohama. There's not much more to do down there but go to Terrapin House."

"I need help with other things. I give you a week."

"And then?" said the expression on Matsu's face. He held his peace.

"Is Lloyd still seeing the woman?"

"The magistrate's office thinks he isn't. He's had a falling out with his boss. Not important enough to report to the consulate or the magistrate's office."

"Poor fellow, when he was having such a good time."

"He'll be better off in England. This place isn't good for young foreigners. It's a swamp. A swamp of—" and Matsu used a crude macho expression for the female generative organ. "I wonder why it isn't for us too."

"We tread with a lighter step. Well, young fellow, I have to see to my hunches. They're getting impatient. One of my hunches takes me to Ryogoku. I could use your vast and detailed knowledge."

"Another reason for getting the case out of the way in a hurry. I don't like being to be seen in Ryogoku with you."

"Thank you."

"You're too famous, is what I meant. Not being famous has its good points."

"Thank you. Well, then."

"Everything fits, except I don't have the weapon."

"In the old days you could have gotten along without one. Well, if you need anybody to bully anybody just let me know."

"You said you wouldn't help with the case."

"Bullying someone the old-fashioned way is different. Well. You to the left and I to the right. Stop by when you have something interesting, or need someone to hold your hand."

"Or do some bullying."

As he set forth in pursuit of hunches, Hanshichi asked where the dancing teacher's temple was. On the precincts would be the grave of the adopted daughter. He had no trouble making sense of the answer, although he was not familiar with the temple in question. It was the little temple with the plastered wall across the street from the big temple, he learned. Everyone knew the big temple. He also asked the posthumous name of the young teacher. It would be on the stone. He did not ask the family name. Since he did not already know it, there probably was none. Genuine family names were the exception in plebeian Edo, although some had acquired designations not blessed by the authorities, who were very snobbish about family names. In that day when people stayed close to home there was little need for them. "The dancing teacher just off the shogun's road" in whatever neighborhood it might be did well enough. Hanshichi himself had visited some of the northern provinces, but the recent walk to Yokohama was the longest he had had in rather a while. Among his neighbors people who had never ventured from the snugness of Edo were not hard to find.

He went out to the Shogun's Road, thinking to go home. Instead he turned back. Soon he was at the big temple and across from it were plastered walls, a rich muddy brown, the best sort of wall, Hanshichi thought. He had not visited the temple before, but he expected to be pleased with it. Inside the gate was a flower stand, with heaps of the magnolia branches that were traditional grave offerings. He bought a bunch, and had no trouble finding the grave. The cemetery was small, shady, mossy, and utterly still. Cemeteries were among the most beautiful places in Edo, and this one was above average. Hanshichi was fond of cemeteries, which, when one tree or another was in blossom, could be among the liveliest places in the city. When only weeds were in bloom, as now, they were good places for meditating on the evanescence of things. Hanshichi had no time just at the moment, but he told himself that he must come and do it. The weeds were of course just weeds, a sign that no one had come weeding recently, but some of them too were very pretty. Hanshichi particularly liked the tiny yellow agronomy flowers. The grave plot too was tiny, though there would be room for the spooky dancing teacher, as apparently there had been for earlier members of the family. The stone suggested without actually saying so that there were such. Ashes from cremations take little room.

Someone else had recently visited the grave. Fresh irises and lilies filled the vase under the tombstone. He crammed his magnolias in, a little ashamed of them. The earlier flowers were better. They showed more careful attention, and they spoke of the season. His flowerless branches spoke of nothing but the most generalized wish to pay heed. A snake slithered by. Could it be—but of course it could not be. He had hunches with regard to the snake as well.

"You're a new one," said the old woman at the flower stand. She probably needed someone to talk to.

"There have been others? I suppose the old dance teacher comes all the time. Was it she that brought the flowers? Not knowing that she would be here so soon herself. It's the way of the world," he added, that being the proper thing to say on such occasions.

"The spooky dance teacher? It would have been better for everyone if she had been put away first. No, she hasn't been here once since the funeral. Plenty of them came just after the funeral. Pupils of the young teacher, I'm sure. A few kept coming every month on the day she died. One young man still does. The young teacher came all the time before she got sick, and she wasn't related to any of them. Of course the old teacher may not have been either. Sometimes the young man was with the young teacher."

Members of a "family" of artists or performers, or gangsters for that matter, were often unrelated to one another.

"Not many young people these days would take the trouble."

"Really Yataro is one of the nicest young men around. He's the son of the paperer out on the Shogun's Road. One of the nicest young men you could hope to meet."

"Papering" was one of the more delicate and genteel of crafts. A paperer mounted sacred texts and works of art, and repaired and replaced the surfaces of sliding doors, some of them also works of art. Most of them were merely paper.

Hanshichi was very slightly acquainted with the young man, whose name he had not known. He had been in the crowd at the mouth of the teacher's alley after the body was discovered.

He thanked the flower woman. What he was really grateful

for was that she did not seem to have recognized him. He went home.

The day being an unseasonably warm one, he had no callers and did not go out. The heat was nothing compared to what would come with full summer, but it took getting used to. A person got sleepy. In the evening the murdered woman's landlord stopped by. The coroner had made his inspection and handed down a preliminary opinion. I was not a very satisfying one. The killer might have been the snake and then again it might not have been. It might have been a human being. Since the victim was distinctly unpopular, someone living or dead could have assumed the form of a snake and done her in. Yes, this was most probably the case.

Hanshichi laughed. It was a stupid world that would accept such a view, and a lazy official who would hand it down. Arrests and prosecutions were not as difficult as they would be if these new-fangled foreign ways came to predominate, but they meant work all the same. There was a type of functionary in the police and justice system who did not do any more than he had to. Snakes that were embodiments of jealousy and resentment tended not to get punished. No reports had to be written, no hearings held. Hearings tended to be brief and of a no-nonsense sort. A core of justice was present, however. The magistrate had to be sure in his (there were no female magistrates) heart that the accused was guilty. Therefore preliminary work had to be done, and the lazy ones would as soon not do it. If guilty suspects sometimes escaped, innocent ones were not often punished.

Hanshichi went to the funeral, which was held the next day at the small temple with the mud walls. The corpse was borne in upon a litter. Thirty or forty people from the neighborhood were in attendance. Hanshichi found a place in a rear corner. Sacred texts were read, each of those present offered leafy branches by way of farewell, and the corpse was taken off to the crematory. The congregation dispersed. Hanshichi was the last to go. He looked closely at each face, seeking to remember as many as he could without resorting to the awkward a device of taking notes.

He saw the paperer's boy and the little serving maid who had worked for the spooky dance teacher.

He went out into the cemetery. Someone was at the grave he had visited the day before. He was not surprised to see that it was Yataro, the paperer's boy. Finding a large tombstone to hide behind, Hanshichi watched. The young man was immersed in prayer. He finished and turned to go, and Hanshichi's head emerged from the tombstone behind him.

"Is there something. . . ." Yataro was confused.

"Yes. There's something I want to ask about. Come over here, please."

Hanshichi led the way back to the grave of the young teacher, soon to be that of the older as well. The two hunkered down in the grass. It was still wet with dew. The sky was overcast.

"I hear you come every month to visit the grave. That is good of you."

Yataro did not ask where he had had these tidings or what business they were of his. Here was evidence that he knew who Hanshichi was.

He answered politely. "I took lessons from the young teacher. We were good friends. There's nothing, really, that needs explaining."

"I won't waste words. We're both of us busy people. Was something going on between you and the young teacher?"

Yataro paled and did not answer. He tugged at the grass under his knees.

"It would be best to tell me the truth. Something was going on between you and the young teacher. And on the anniversary the old teacher did it too, and they both of them did it in an unhappy way. A coincidence, you might say. But there's more to it than that. People are saying that you did something to the old teacher to get even for the young teacher. That's what people are saying, and the constable's office has heard about it."

"Why would they be talking about me? Why?" The young man was very upset. His lip was trembling.

"I know you didn't do it. I'm just telling you what people are saying, and I'm doing it for your own good. You may have recognized me and you've probably heard of me. My name's Hanshichi. I live over there and do police work. I'm not the kind to take gossip seriously and run up an innocent man. And you can pay me back by telling me everything you know. Everything, nothing left out. The young teacher is in this grave. You wouldn't want to tell lies in front of her, now, would you."

The lilies and iris, fresh the day before, were wilting. Yataro stared at the wilting leaves. There were tears in his eyes.

"All right. I'll tell you everything. A couple of years ago I started going for lessons almost every night. The young teacher—you have to believe me. I never did anything wrong. The young teacher was not in good health, as you know, and I'm not the boldest person around. All we did was have a good talk now and then when the old teacher's wasn't watching. There was one time in particular. It was in the spring, last year. The young teacher said there were reasons why she couldn't go on living in that house. Wouldn't I run off with her somewhere. Now that I know what I know I think I should have done it. But I had my family to think about and I couldn't just run off with a woman. So I persuaded her to go home. Very soon afterwards she took to her bed, and you know the rest. I can't get over feeling that I killed her. And so I never miss a month. I go to the grave and apologize to her. That's all there is. I had nothing at all to do with the old teacher's death. The story of how she died surprised me as much as it did anyone. And it happened exactly on the anniversary. They called her the spooky teacher. She really was."

It was as Hanshichi had suspected. Relations between the two young people made a sad love story. The young man was weeping. Hanshichi was sure that he was telling the truth.

"And after the young teacher died you stopped taking lessons and you haven't been in the house since?"

"Yes."

This was a clear enough answer. It meant that the suppositions behind the questions were correct. But Yataro seemed to swallow the word.

"You're not to hold anything back. It's too important. You really haven't been in the place since the young teacher died?"

"Well, actually." Yataro hesitated. "As a matter of fact there was something very peculiar."

"What was it? The longer you wait the worse it will be. Come on now. Let's have it."

Yataro fidgeted. With Hanshichi glaring at him, he finally gathered the necessary resolve. It must have been about a month after the young teacher's death, he said. The old teacher stopped by the papering shop. She asked Yataro to come outside. She wanted to discuss arrangements for the thirty-fifth day, she said. Would he mind coming around in the evening? Buddhist conventions required prayers every week after a death until, on the forty-ninth day, it might be hoped that the departed spirit had found a new home. Arrangements for the fifth of the seven weekly observances were only her excuse. What she really wanted to talk about was what he thought peculiar. When he had heard the story, Hanshichi had to agree.

Might she ask him to let her adopt him as her son? Desperately lonely since the death of her adopted daughter, she wanted to adopt another daughter or a son. He was the favored candidate.

This was wholly unexpected. He was oldest son and heir in his own family. He of course refused. She did not give up easily. She was constantly after him to come over for advice and consultation. One afternoon she apprehended him out on the street and took him to a teahouse in the Yushima hills west of the Kanda and Shitaya flatlands. He was a teetotaller, but she forced sake on him. She drank amply herself, and as she got drunk her proposal changed. She no longer wanted to adopt him, she wanted to marry him. Or so it seemed. He was not quite sure. Her manner now was most seductive. Yataro fled.

Hanshichi laughed. "And when did this happen?"

"During the New Year holidays. Then in March I ran into her in Asakusa. She tried to take me off somewhere, but I got away from her. A while afterwards, I think it must have been towards the end of March, I went to the bathhouse. I came out of the men's bath and bumped into her coming out of the women's. She said she had something to talk to me about.

"I couldn't very well refuse. So I went off with her to her house. She slid the inside door open and a man was sitting in the parlor, a man with a dark skin, maybe forty, seven or eight years younger than the teacher. She seemed very surprised. She just stood there. I turned and ran off."

Hanshichi was still smiling. "You have no idea who the man was?"

"None at all. Mura said they had a fight and he went off mad."

Mura was the maid.

It seemed that Yataro had nothing more to say. Hanshichi cut the interview short, and they went their separate ways.

"Don't say anything to anybody about our little conversation till I tell you you can. I know you didn't do it. That's what matters. Just keep quiet."

On his way home, he ran into Matsu.

"I wouldn't want to take you out of your way," said Hanshichi, when they had exchanged remarks about the weather, which went on being warm, "but I'd like to go to Ryogoku with you some time when you're going."

"As a matter of fact I'm on my way there now. I stopped by and found out from the lady at your house where you'd been and thought I might run into you. But I didn't expect you to want to Ryogoku with me. You know where it is as well as I do."

"Not today. Next time. It's a little hot, and I always want a bath after a funeral."

"You could make do with tossing a little salt around. Didn't they give you salt?"

They had of course given everyone a packet of salt. They always did at a funeral. It was the universal purifier.

"Tossing salt around might make me cleaner but it won't make me feel any cleaner. Next time."

"Why do you want to go to Ryogoku?"

"Do you still see men selling good-luck charms?"

"Of course. Women too. Every shrine has them. You must know that."

"I was thinking of the ones that work the streets. The traveling salesmen. Ryogoku used to be the place for them."

"I don't know. I haven't been much interested."

"You must learn to be interested in all aspects of the world around you. You can't know when one of them might be useful."

"All aspects. That's quite a few. Does it have something to do with the spooky dancer?"

"Dance teacher, actually. She never was much of a dancer. My life is centered upon her, these days, sort of."

# 7

Ryogoku was at the two approaches, eastern and western, to the bridge of the same name, the oldest of four bridges across the Sumida. The eastern approach had in recent decades become the liveliest, for a boathouse owned and used by Lord Tokugawa himself had had a subduing effect on the other. It was the busiest place east of the river and one of several "broad alleys" scattered over the plebeian flatlands.

The expression "broad alley" was something of a contradiction, alleys being narrow things, but this did not bother children of Edo. They did not know much about foreign languages, and lived peaceably enough with contradictions in their own language. A few scholarly types did know an amount of Chinese. Every neighborhood had its scholar, and he could assure those who were interested that Chinese too was full of contradictions.

Hanshichi did indeed have good reason for visiting Ryogoku. He did not want to bother himself much longer with the case of the spooky dance teacher, and Ryogoku seemed the best place to go in search of a solution. Besides, he liked it, and worried about it.

Of the several broad alleys that he knew, the eastern Ryogoku one was the least inhibited and the most isolated. The new day was not likely to be kind to it. Occasionally, at the constable's offices or some similar place, he would hear talk of the government's thoughts about accommodating this new day. The watery lowlands along the river would be a good place for the factories which the country needed if it was to survive. This meant that they would remain working-class districts and share little in the riches which, he was told, the new day would bring. Ryogoku was a part of the flatlands almost certain to lose its vitality. Hanshichi was sorry, although he did not object to catching up with the world and perhaps even driving the barbarians away.

With considerable uniformity, the broad alleys of Edo lay beside or in front of famous and popular religious establishments. In the Ryogoku case it was the Ekoin, a Buddhist temple established to honor and remember victims of the greatest fire in the history of the city. Several hundred thousand of them (Hanshichi had heard and did not doubt) had reached the river bank and been able to go no farther. When the flames subsided the bodies were ferried across the river for cremation and entombment.

So the Ekoin came to be, and, as well, the big variety show stretched out along the river before it. A most excellent thing about the latter, thought Hanshichi and even more Matsu, was that a person was not required to spend money. The performers were mostly peddlers and mendicants. They would have liked a few pennies, or the Edo equivalent, but only the more complex enterprises, such as little theaters, charged fees. Even with them admission charges were sometimes foresworn. Donations were collected, as at a religious ceremony.

The disaster occurred in the Seventeenth Century, when Edo was still a raw, uncultured place. To be the greatest of its fires was no small feat. Edo was famous for fires. Hanshichi had seen some splendid ones. It was because of the disaster that Lord Tokugawa grudgingly allowed Ryogoku Bridge to be built. He did not like big bridges. He thought that they invited incursions. It was almost a century since the newest bridge had been put across the river.

In fact the incursion went the other way. Because of the bridge the regions east of the river began to develop and became parts of Edo. The boundaries of the province in which Edo reposed were moved to a river or two east of the Sumida. Kanda being near the center of the city they approached from the west. The west might have been an interesting enough place had the east not beckoned. It had good views across the river and on to the plains and the highest mountain of the east country. It had musical and dramatic performances in flimsy little theaters, neither the quality nor the prices the best in town. It had pretty girls in charge of drinking places and what were ostensibly archery stalls. No one who had reached the age of reason could possibly want the trumpery that was offered as prizes for skillful archery. Every adult Edo male, however matters may have been with old women from remote provinces, knew that the pretty girls offered other services. These were more open in the drinking places than in the archery places, but they were thinly concealed in the latter places as well.

The east bank awaited them. Even the view across the river announced it to be the livelier of the banks. The count of streamers was much higher, and each streamer offered something to see or something to buy. From the main gate of the temple on up the river was a solid flow of them, dancing merrily in the spring breeze. They sounded a silent welcome.

Hanshichi and Matsu had their choice between walking across the bridge and taking a boat. Without consulting Matsu Hanshichi chose the boat. Interesting things were always happening on boats, and Hanshichi preferred old devices. He feared that even as the new day would do away with the pleasures of Ryogoku it would do away with the ferries. All the young people who made the big difference in the spirit of a place would be coursing along on horses or in vehicles pulled by them. The ferries did not accommodate horses.

From the ferry they could hear the crowds on the eastern bank. Prominent among the sounds drifting out over the river was religious chanting. Every chanter would have liked a few pennies. To give to all of them would cost a fortune, and Hanshichi (he did not speak for Matsu) did not mean to give to any of them. He did not approve of mendicancy. Let a fellow work for a living.

Most of the other passengers were women with packages, probably gifts, in pretty kerchiefs. They were probably on their way to call on siblings and parents.

Near the prow two men of middle years were having an argument.

"An argument is always worth eavesdropping on," said Hanshichi, moving closer. "Especially a warm one."

This argument was very warm indeed. One man was accusing the other of making off with something. He wanted the object back. That was all he wanted. It was not clear whether the object had been borrowed or stolen.

The ambiguity gave Hanshichi his opening, not that he needed one. All he really needed was a look of authority.

"If he took something that didn't belong to him why don't you go to the police?"

"What good would that do?"

"Sometimes it does good, sometimes it doesn't. Isn't that the way in this world?"

"What business is it of yours?"

"Everything is my business."

Hanshichi assumed his bureaucratic mien, very threatening. Generally it was all he needed. Even if he had announced himself as an agent of the shogun he would not have been asked to show identification. His business was made easier by the fact that he worked mostly with townsmen, who tended to be cooperative. Matsu looked on in silent meditation. He would have had to cultivate a bureaucratic manner himself but for the fact that the time for such things was running out. And but for the fact that he was not at all sure he was up to it.

"What are your names? Where do you live?"

"What business is it of yours?" repeated the man, the one who had been the agent of the unidentified loss.

The bureaucratic mien had not worked ideally well. It was a trifle embarrassing that something more specific was called for.

"Everything is the shogun's business." And indeed it was, though Matsu was probably right that this would change.

The other man, he who had suffered the unidentified loss, was for obvious reasons willing to cooperate. He identified himself, to the extent that identification was possible. Sons and daughters of Edo, frequently lacking family names, identified themselves by residence, occupation, and the like.

And of course by surnames. This man was named Saburo.

Hanshichi looked at Matsu, who shook his head. This was

not Lloyd's friend, or acquaintance, the Yokohama Saburo. Which was all right. Saburo, "Third Son," was the commonest of masculine names.

There was a similar trouble with addresses. They tended to be not very specific. Everyone in a neighborhood knew where everyone else lived, and on most occasions that was all that mattered. The nearest this man could come to an address was a sort of projection based on somewhat prominent stationary objects such as bridges and temples. Forbidden for the most part in the center of the city, temples and cemeteries were numerous on the outskirts. The watery lands east of the river were well provided with bridges, which were helpful. Lord Tokugawa may have frowned on bridges across the Sumida, but no one was likely to attack anyone over a bridge across a canal. The reaction of the other man informed Hanshichi that the information was not inaccurate.

"And you?" he asked the other.

The other was a harder case. He refused to answer. This provided Hanshichi with the valuable information that he had something to hide.

Hanshichi looked very fierce and very magisterial, but to no effect.

"Well, here we are," said Hanshichi. "Wish it had been a longer trip, but it isn't much of a river, when you think about it. I'll detain the two of you for just a bit, shogun's business, you know, while my young helper here runs off and gets some vinegar. You know where to get it, of course."

Matsu did not look entirely sure, but it did not matter. In panic, the recalcitrant man gave name and residence. Hanshichi, glanced at the other, the good guy, so to speak. He nodded.

"Thank you. That's all for now. Oh. Just one second more." With great solemnity he wrote down such information as he had obtained about names and addresses. The two men agreed as to their accuracy. "May I trouble you to tell the shogun's representative, which is me, what the missing object is, or was?"

"Something no sensible person would want to have, and most would want to be rid of as soon as possible." This was from the more cooperative of the two men.

"A rat. A cockroach. A pigeon. A snake. A mother-in-law. And of these the most likely are a snake and a mother-in-law."

"Only a woman would have mother-in-law trouble," said Matsu. "And it is my strong impression that neither of these gentleman is a woman"

Hanshichi smiled. He was right, of course. In the Japanese family it was most commonly women who had mother-in-law trouble. This was because the man's mother lived with the younger couple, and so, except in instances where a man was adopted into his wife's family. it was the younger woman who had the trouble. But he had put together his list as a joke. Neither of the men commented upon it, and so most probably the lost object was a snake.

"And what was that about"

Hanshichi had not objected when the quarreling men moved on.

"What was what about? Is there anything that wasn't perfectly clear?"

"What was the vinegar thing about? I think I could have found some for you, but I was glad you seemed to lose interest. I would have felt a little silly."

"You've never seen vinegar used to enforce the shogun's law, whatever that might be?"

Matsu looked deeply humiliated.

"Things are going to pieces in a big hurry, but that's not your fault. Anyway, I'm sure you've noticed, who wouldn't, that this beautiful weather has brought the mosquitoes out. Has it struck you as odd that there is a proverb about the bad wind the bucket-maker profits from but not the beautiful sunshine that brings pests?"

"I think about it all the time."

"I suppose it's another thing the new day will do away with, but there has been a little trick to make someone talk when he doesn't want to. It only works in good mosquito weather. You make him take off his clothes, and I suppose getting a criminal to strip is another thing that will go out of fashion. It' s easy enough.

A threat or two usually takes care of it. And vinegar and the mosquitoes, and the fellow will do anything to get rid of them. I don't know why mosquitoes like vinegar, but they do. I don't know why we children of Edo like it either, but we do."

It was true that the only dish, or very nearly the only one, at which Edo was better than the big cities of the west was centered on vinegar.

The two of them first paid their respects at the main hall of the temple. Then they looked to see how preparations for the spring Sumo tournament were coming. The Ekoin was the place where the biggest and most important tournaments were held. Quite as they had expected, stands of bamboo and reeds were going up. These were very flimsy, and would come back down again once the tournament was over. A grand tournament lasted for ten days, but they were not usually successive ones. Matches were called off on rainy days. The stands offered better protection against sun than against rain. Since the only people who feared sun in this clement season were professional women whose fair complexions were a necessary part of their business, there might as well have been no stands at all.

Hanshichi was a very conservative man. He did not think that the new day would do anyone much good. He was also an open-minded man, however, and he was willing to recognize exceptions. The sports of the men of the western seas would be a big improvement over traditional sports. He had observed team sports down in Yokohama, and thought that the clever, nimble-fingered son of Edo would be improved by them. He especially liked the one, American, it was said, played by several men with a stick and a ball. At any rate the son of Edo deserved better than Sumo, which, when among friends he could trust, Hanshichi usually described as stupid. He recognized that it was a part of Edo that could not easily be cut away, but the son of Edo, who tended to be small and slender, deserved something nearer his own proportions than enormously fat men pushing one another out of rings.

Still he was glad to see that preparations went on apace. The constable could probably get tickets for him if he wanted them.

He would think about it. Going through the tea houses that had a monopoly on tickets for a more ordinary sort of clientele was altogether too much of a bother; but, whether you liked the sport or not, an outdoor afternoon with good friends and plenty to drink was a not unpleasant way to spend a spring afternoon.

Before they left the main temple grounds they stopped by the most famous grave in the cemetery. Temple grounds always had cemeteries. It was the grave of a robber who had been put to death a quarter of a century earlier. His popular name was Rat Boy. This had to do with his agility and small stature. He was able to get into and out of a house not his own with the skill of a rat. Along with Sumo, the grave was the biggest attraction the temple had to offer. The position of the good priests seemed to be that even a criminal deserved a chance at salvation. Again, it may have been that every visitor put down a little money. Hanshichi and Matsu did.

"So here we are paying our respects to the enemy," said Hanshichi. "Pretty broad-minded of us, is what I say."

"Not our enemy. Theirs," said Matsu, gesturing broadly in the direction of the castle and the hills behind it.

"An enemy of Lord Tokugawa," said Hanshichi, solemnly, "is an enemy of all of us." He smiled a solemn smile.

"If you say so."

Rat Boy was a Robin Hood figure in popular lore. He robbed only the mansions of the rich and powerful, and he was very generous towards the poor and weak. Or so the lore had it. The first half of the statement was unquestionably true. Everyone knew of noble mansions he had broken into, no one of a townsman's abode. It was a noble mansion that was his undoing. In spite of his skills, he was caught and beheaded. The second half was more doubtful.

If the temple welcomed criminals unto its bosom, it also welcomed sinners of another kind. The eastern stretches in which it lay had the largest number of unlicensed prostitutes in the city. Along the river bank a little downstream from the temple gold cats and silver cats plied their trade. They were called cats because the samisen was the symbol of the pleasure quarters and catskin was very important among its ingredients. Gold cats were of course more expensive than silver ones.

The Yoshiwara, the main licensed quarter of the city, up the river above Asakusa, was always burning down. It had done so several times in recent years. After a fire, the licensed prostitutes found temporary places of business here and there, mostly in the eastern part of the city. Ryogoku was such a place. Having taken up temporary residence they seemed to think they might as well stay a while. The distinction between licensed and unlicensed prostitution was gradually blurred. The market became freer, so to speak. Always on the side of the son of Edo, Hanshichi approved.

Of the two broad alleys, at either approach to the bridge, the eastern one, almost everyone agreed, and certainly Hanshichi did, was the more interesting. The one to the west, on the opposite side of the river, was older, and because of Lord Tokugawa's boathouse had taken on a certain dignity. This was not what the son of Edo had in mind when he went out in search of entertainment. The eastern one had come to bustle more, and was much the more raffish.

Leaving the temple behiind. Hanshichi and Matsu moved up river, along the tunnel of streamers.

"The best show in town," said Hanshichi, "and if it's the best show in this town it's the best in the country. The best in the world, maybe. I hope I'm still around when things open up and we can go have a look at the world."

"I wouldn't know what to wear."

Matsu's first purchase was some tooth powder. By the time they had finished their walk he had to buy a kerchief to tie up his purchases in. It was a severely handsome kerchief, in the masculine Edo style, not the frivolously and somewhat gaudily feminine (or so the son of Edo thought) Kyoto style.

"Just learning how to do it must take years. And somebody has to do some teaching. Which means it's been going on for a long time. And makes you wonder who invented it, and when."

Lost in contemplation of this marvel, Hanshichi bought some

powder too. "I think it's probably just salt, but that's all right. It's the spirit of the thing."

"What I wanted to say. You say things so much better. How do you suppose he gets up there? And down again."

"You don't know? I suppose you don't come here very often. Too far east for young fellows like you. You'll see in a minute. He may be on top of things, but he can't stay there for very long."

The object of their admiration had mounted a stool balanced atop a single leg on another which was similarly mounted on yet another. On top of the uppermost stool he was engaged in strenuous sword play, drawing a sword from a scabbard, cutting down an imagined enemy, reinserting it without looking at the scabbard.

"Looks like a real sword, too. I wonder where he got it."

"Things are going to pieces."

Commoners were not supposed to have swords. Of course there was a slim possibility that the man was not a commoner. Many a person of the warrior classes was, these days, in reduced circumstances. That things were going to pieces, one way and another, was not to be denied. Hanshichi was not inclined to inquire whether possession of the sword was legal or not.

"Now, then," said Hanshichi, as an older man came up beside the column of stools on which a youngish man was performing.

The younger stepped to the older man's shoulders. The older man squatted down and let the other descend to the ground. Then they reversed positions. The younger man stood up and the older stepped to the top of the column. They probably were in some such relationship as teacher and disciple. Whatever, it was teamwork of a very high order.

The two men were not alone among peddlers who showed remarkable skill. There was a man who flung noodles high into the air and caught them with chopsticks as they came down. There was a man who flung coins into the air and caught them on the tip of a straw. There was a man who balanced himself on his head without the support of arms and hands. There he was, standing on his head with arms folded before him. He used arms and hands to get into position, then dispensed with them.

There was a man who played a samisen which he held on top of his head. There was a man who leaped through a basketwork tube lined with knife points, and emerged without a scratch.

There were mendicants in large numbers, all of them in religious garb, many of them chanting and banging and clanging. The din had increased as they crossed the river.

"I see that you draw the line somewhere," he said, observing that Matsu made no contributions.

"They have other ways of supporting themselves."

Hanshichi thought that this made great good sense.

There was an exception, a man in priestly garb who was beating on a drum with a huge wooden phallus. Matsu dropped a couple of coins at his feet. So did Hanshichi, though his timing suggested that he would not have done it had he been alone.

"I've heard about him," said Hanshichi. "He doesn't like women."

"He wouldn't have many women in his audience anyway. But I'll bet a few of them take a peek."

The crowds were overwhelmingly masculine. Women did not go out by themselves, and husbands were embarrassed to be seen with their wives.

Afternoon was the best time. The son of Edo was an early riser but he was also a hard worker. There came a time in the afternoon when it was not embarrassing to be seen at one of the broad alleys. The evenings tended to be quiet because of the terrible danger of fire in a crowded city built almost entirely of wood.

There were dramatic monologues and more properly dramatic performances. Matsu gave a little money to the ones who worked hardest, such as a solitary performer doing all the roles, male and female.

There were dog shows and monkey shows. Hanshichi remembered having seen a camel, when he was a small boy, at this same Ryogoku. Its urine, held to be medicinal, was on sale. Brought in by the Dutch through Nagasaki, the camel was very popular. Though he had seen exotic beasts from places nearer at hand, tigers and such, he had not seen another camel. It was a male camel. There had been talk of importing a female camel, to see what they might do together (here in the shadow of the great temple), but it had not come. There was no camel today, male or female, but there were brightly colored tropical birds, and there were remarkable four-footed performers of famous Kabuki roles.

Freaks were numerous. Some were grotesque. There were monstrously tall men and monstrously fat women and dwarfs, called spider men, whose heads were larger than all the rest of them. There was a bear woman, not quite as hairy as a bear but not far from it. One very tall man had a neck so twisted that he was always looking over a shoulder. He was said to have been the victim of an encounter with a horse. There were people with abnormally large numbers of limbs and digits.

There were persons with strange habits, a young woman, for instance, said to live on raw dog entrails. Indeed there she was, mouth all bloody, chewing away. Getting a grip on his stomach and approaching close, Hanshichi was inclined to think that the flesh, though raw and far from appetizing, especially for someone who acceded to Buddhist tenets about the eating of flesh, was that of a chicken, and that the blood was not real. The young woman was rather pretty, behind all the gore. Another woman seemed to have testicles, though probably they were something else. There was a man who could break wind incessantly and in rhythm. There was a man who could pop his eyes out and put them back in, ready to pop again, apparently no worse for the experience. He could do it in rhythm and suspend objects from them. There was a man with a hole in his stomach. He used it for smoking tobacco. There were people who swallowed impossible objects, such as swords and tobacco pipes. Those with a taste for such things were invited to see the object in question emerging from the anus.

Hanshichi reached for a feel, which was not permitted.

"Aren't you going to tell him you're on the shogun's business?"

"And get the shogun in trouble?"

"It's rubber. But how did it get there?"

Because of the part the snake had played in the death of the dance teacher, Hanshichi was especially interested in the handlers of snakes, charmers and the like. There was an element of the erotic in the snake charming. Some of the charmers were scantily dressed young women. One extraordinary young woman would insert a small snake into her mouth and bring it out through an ear. It was a small black snake, closely resembling the one which superstitious people thought had done the teacher in.

Hanshichi reached over as if to pat it on the head. The owner objected.

"On the shogun's business," said Matsu, though by no means as sternly as Hanshichi would have. Maybe he was getting ready for the new age.

"See?" said Hanshichi.

"Yes. See what? It was a little black snake."

"Very much like the one on the dance teacher."

"I don't know much about snakes. But yes, I'd say so."

"With one big difference."

Matsu waited.

"It didn't bow."

"I beg your pardon?"

"It didn't pull its head away. The other one did. That wasn't natural. It had been trained. Well, I'll head back into the sunset. I'm sure you can guess what I want you to do."

"Find out as much as I can about the argument on the boat."

"Exactly."

# 8

The day was a fine one and Hanshichi always began to think there was something wrong with him when he had not done much walking. His legs and digestive tract would start berating him for his indolence.

Nor did he feel that he was wasting valuable time. His two current cases, that of the severed alien head and that of the dance teacher, were dormant. He could do little but wait for something to happen. No new case had come up recently. Sometimes he was investigating a half dozen cases simultaneously, but the city, or at any rate this plebeian part of it, seemed to be comporting itself well these days. Probably it only seemed so. These were times of great uncertainty, with barbarians at the gates, or the ports.

Hanshichi liked the narrow band east of the river that could be said to belong to the city. Beyond it lay open lands, where farmers and fishermen pursued their trades. This district where the urban and rural came together was popular with all of Edo for excursions. Many-a famous tree and grove and garden attracted them, and they liked the sense of liberation which the verdant flatlands gave them, and the views to distant mountains, most conspicuous of them Fuji, in the west.

It could not have been said that he had wholly left business behind. He always had it on his mind. Edo was an interesting city, and a person never knew what he would run into in the course of a walk. He wished to check on the addresses they had had from the men on the ferry, and especially that of the man who had been more likely to be telling the truth and would be more likely to cooperate. He might provide Matsu, whose imagination could stand developing, something to work on.

He took a discursive route, now eastwards and now westwards, in a generally northerly direction, and recrossed the river by Azuma Bridge, the one next north from Ryogoku Bridge. Azuma bridge meant something like "bridge of the east" or "bridge to the east." Neither made complete sense, since all of Edo was held by the haughty ones of the western cities to belong to the rough, uncouth east, and since the roads eastwards from it did not lead much of anywhere at all. That was not worth worrying about. One did not ask that pleasant place names make complete sense. Azuma was the newest of the bridges across the Sumida.

He came several times, in his meanderings, to the eastern limits of the city. Beyond lay paddy lands and in the distant north and west mountains. Fuji to the west was much the highest and most famous, but Hanshichi preferred the more modest Tsukuba to the north. It was of the East Country. Fuji lay beyond the most threatening of Lord Tokugawa's barriers and was not.

These eastern limits of the city were rather different from the southern ones through which Hanshichi and Matsu had passed on their way to Yokohama. The latter were neither urban nor rural, and indicated the direction into which the former wished to expand. Here in the east the division between the two was clear. He could not of course predict what the city, with all its vagaries, would decide to do, but they seemed more securely rural. Like many a son and daughter of the crowded plebeian parts of the city, Hanshichi preferred them and chose them for excursions. His sister had chosen the north for her cherry-blossom excursion, because that was what everyone in the neighborhood did. Here in the east there were not the massed blossoms that invited blossom-viewing abandon. Those he had had at Shinagawa. Yet it was largely blossoms, and not verdant paddies or distant mountains, that brought people east of the river, often in large groups.

It was not considered effeminate for the sturdy son of Edo to like flowers. Hanshichi did not dislike cherries. A variety recently developed in the northern outskirts of Edo was driving out older forms and becoming the favorite for springtime revelers the whole land over, even the royal capital. It seemed a little grand and haughty, however. Other blossoms seemed more on his level.

A few steps north of the Ekoin was a wall, a next to interminable wall. It was pleasing enough to the eye, but it demanded a wide detour. It enclosed a watery zone, essentially inlets from the river, where Lord Tokgawa kept his stocks of bamboo. Hanshichi had no notion why Lord Tokugawa required such quantities of bamboo. Perhaps he gave it to his friends. The detour did not discommode Hanshichi. It took him the better part of the way to the eastern limits of the city, and he would have wanted to go there anyway. Of the wavering line where city gave way to country he had only pleasant recollections. It may not have had cherries in great profusion, but it had all the other blossoms of the seasons. He had been on many an excursion to view this one and that one. Excursions tended to be in the clement seasons, and an alcoholic haze enveloped them.

He especially liked plums. There were famous ones along the line, such as an aged tree called the reclining one, because branches were so remote from the trunk that some of them touched the ground. Very near it was a pond famous for wisteria bowers. The time of the plum had passed, at the end of winter and the beginning of spring, but wisteria, another favorite, was at its best. Both places carried associations with a statesman of a millennium or so before who had been treated badly by the jealous ones in charge of the royal court. In a sense, though actual power over the land reposed in Edo, its sons and daughters had received similar treatment. They were always being put in their place by the haughty ones of the west. Hanshichi thought the bowers before him called for a drink, and had one. He thought the day a success, though thus far it had been without striking successes.

On one of his turns back towards the river he found the address of the more cooperative participant in the ferry altercation. It was one of a cluster of cheap inns. The man was probably an itinerant peddler, one of those who walked the country (literally walked), and who either had no permanent residence or were not in it very much. Hanshichi thought such people very brave and deserving of every tiny coin they made. Some of them, as one in Hanshichi's business knew all too well, may have cheated a bit, but who could expect them all to behave impeccably? Hanshichi was inclined to think that even fraud if pursued unswervingly might be not far from a virtue. It was a sentiment he would not have dreamed of giving voice to in the presence of the constable by the river.

Hanshichi would not have hesitated to identify himself and ask a few questions if it had seemed necessary. It did not. Sometimes a person could literally sniff out important information. Hanshichi caught a reptilian odor, offensively pungent, as if to serve warning. Here was something to report to Matsu. In the world of the itinerant peddler, persons who pursued similar callings tended to congregate. It was a way of keeping up with things and spying upon their fellows. He would have expressed the thought without reference to birds and feathers, for his was a language that did not pay much attention to rhyme, possibly because, with its paucity of vowels, everything rhymed already.

Back on the west side of the Sumida, he was at the great Asakusa Temple. It was generally considered the best of the great Edo variety shows. He did not exactly hurry past it, but he did not loiter. One big temple in a day was enough. This was not to say that they were all alike.

In Asakusa he would have found somewhat pricier offerings than in Ryogoku. After a review of the latter he was in a mood for something quieter and more thoughtful. He knew the Asakusa Temple, in any case, better than the Ryogoku one. He was returning from it when he came upon the case of the dance teacher.

With minor detours the walk from the bridge back to Kanda took him through artisan quarters of which he was fond. The little factories were open to the street and sometimes used a part or all of a street for working space. Being watched did not seem to make the workmen nervous. So he watched, sometimes from a distance of only a foot or two.

He loved watching things of delicacy and beauty emerge from the horny hands of workmen. There was a back street occupied exclusively by makers of stencils for dyeing kimono fabrics. He would not have denied that he had prejudices, and one of them favored the crafts of Edo over the flashier ones of Kyoto. The best Edo dyeing was called *komon*, "fine pattern," the adjective to be understood as conveying minuteness. Small patterns, natural or abstract, often showing great powers of observation, were repeated over and over, the repetitions apparent only on close scrutiny. Frequently in a single color, the favorite being indigo, they were never in bright colors. Kyoto fabrics often struck Hanshichi as gaudy. It was a matter of taste. What was undeniable was that the patterns were imaginative and delicate. Stencils for such cloths were what he saw emerging from not at all delicate hands. He thought that here he had the very best of Edo, and the men who produced it were of his own class, and not of the aristocracy in and beyond the castle.

Another street was occupied by carvers of wood blocks for printing. Some were for the polychrome pictures of nature and of man so popular with the Edo commoner, who generally had money for them, since they cost almost nothing. Some were of high quality and some not so much so. Hanshichi had acquaintances who specialized in pornography and were sometimes in trouble with Hanshichi's fellow police persons. He thought this unjust. They were only making a living, and if they had not done it someone else would have, for there was a demand.

He could, if he had the time and the inclination, have inspected their current work. They knew that he would not arrest them. Today he did not have the time, whatever may have been the inclination. Most of the workers were at work at blocks for the printed word. Japan had once had metal type, borrowed from China, but for some reason had discarded it for wood blocks, a block per page. The workmen did not do the calligraphy, but they carved most expertly from texts indited by others. Hanshichi did not know why metal, clearly more convenient, had been discarded in favor of wood, but he sometimes thought that his city had a particular affinity with wood. It was a place of carpenters. It was made of wood and was always burning down.

There was many another street that he could have looked at, one occupied by makers of dolls, one occupied by makers of ceramics, indeed streets for all the craftsmen who supplied the shops and markets of Edo. Inevitably, and Hanshichi wished it were not so, the city looked elsewhere, and especially to the great western metropolises, Osaka and Kyoto, for many of its supplies: inevitably because it contained a huge and unproductive bureaucracy and aristocracy.

Hanshichi liked the wares which Edo produced for itself best, and he especially admired the cutters of stencils and the carvers of woodblocks.

The scene about him was very different from the aristocratic region in which the house of the morning glories reposed. Very wealthy people lived in the plebeian parts of the city, for there were very wealthy merchants. It was not these northern reaches of the flatlands they lived in, however. They had their expansive mansions and gardens behind walls in Nihombashi. There was not a walled garden all up and down the streets Hanshichi passed through. In a sense, however, the streets themselves were gardens. They were lined with potted plants. No house was without these.

The morning glory was the especial favorite. Hanshichi was not much given to philosophical meditation on such points, but the reason seemed obvious. The morning glory was the best symbol of the delicious evanescence of life, and the Edo townsman, though he did not talk about it much, was keenly aware of this. It was true that the morning glory now so popular was a fairly recent import from China, but other flowers had over the centuries borne the name, and they had all been popular, and had in common a rapid blooming and fading.

Hanshichi was sure that Matsu would be coming around and wanted to be at home to receive him. So he did not loiter. He exchanged greetings with a number of craftsmen whom he considered friends and was on his way.

Matsu did not come around until evening. He had stayed on at Ryogoku.

"I hope you enjoyed yourself."

"That's the sort of thing you would say. I was working."

"On which of our many cases?"

"The Yokohama one. The case of the headless body, or the

bodiless head, whichever you prefer. It's not that big a place. I thought I might come on some trace of Saburo. But I'm beginning to think I shouldn't waste any more time on the case."

"You don't have the right spirit."

"Lots of cases go unsolved. You know that better than I do. We may not shout to the world about it, but it's a fact. And we have better excuses with this one than with most of them."

Hanshichi waited for more.

"It's all mixed up with foreigners and the unequal treaties. And pawnbrokers."

"People no one likes or gives a damn about."

"In other words it's a waste of time."

"Oh dear me no. Would I have put you to work on a waste of time? But it would be no disgrace to decide that there are better ways to use your time. That's up to you. And if I don't give you a scolding for it the constable won't."

"Maybe. But maybe he doesn't realize how much time I've put into it."

"And learned a lot I'm sure that will be useful in the new age. And maybe had a few pleasant evenings. And maybe had some effect on the treaties. You can be proud of yourself."

"Especially for the evenings. And what all did you do out by the paddies?"

"Do you know what a snake smells like?"

"I'd imagine there are as many smells as there are kinds of snake. Now you aren't going to make me go sniffing after snakes, are you? Nobody told me when I got into this work that I might need a good nose. I have a terrible one. I never know whether I stink or not."

"It doesn't much matter whether you have a nose for snakes. I do. I caught the smell of them over there. I suppose that was the most important thing I did."

"Congratulations. There are so many smells over there to drown it out."

"You don't seem much interested. Well, the case of the dancing teacher is one we can't drop. It's too close to home. People may not much care what happens to foreigners, but they do care about what happens to their neighbors, as long as they aren't pawnbrokers. A great many people cared about the teacher's daughter."

"And almost everyone seems to think it's a closed case."

"The daughter was very popular. People will be pleased to find out that they were wrong and it wasn't she that did it. Of course you remember the two who had the little falling out on the good old Ryogoku ferry?"

"The one that was accused of taking something much better than the one that had it taken. He looked like a type we might be having business with some day."

"That's too bad. It's the other one you're more likely to run into. I think he probably lives where I caught the snake smell. Here. I drew you a map. It might be a good idea to take the next ferry north. Otherwise you'll have all that bamboo to get past. If you run into the one that had the thing taken be polite to him. If you run into the other, don't. And don't be timid about using the old methods. Not being able to use them down in Yokohama is another good reason for dropping the case."

"I've said it before and I'll say it again, and you must excuse me, because it's important. You're old enough to get by with old-fashioned methods. Some of us are going to have to start learning something else. Have you heard that we are going to have something called a court of law?"

"I don't pay much attention. Tell me about it."

"What it means is that we won't have the last say. Someone else's nose will be poking its way in and it could cost a fellow his job. Anyway. You were speaking of the two men on the ferry."

"I have a feeling that the man who had something taken lives there among the snakes, and it was a snake he had taken. I'm more interested in the other, the one that took the snake or whatever. Either one will do. I want you to 'go hunting. It would be a good idea to get in touch with the boys over there before you do anything else."

When an order was this specific Matsu never said no. "I'll get to it right away. Maybe this evening."

"I think evening might be a good time. People generally come home for dinner. Maybe not home exactly, but you know what I mean.'

Hanshichi went to the paper-mounting place. He was sure that he would find Yasaburo there, for Yasaburo was a good industrious young man. Not surprisingly, Yasaburo did not seem happy to see him.

"Don't let me take you away from what you're doing, but maybe when you're finished I could ask you a few things. I said before that I know you didn't do it and I'll say it again."

Yasaburo was still not happy, but he put aside the paper he was mounting. It was a darkly Chinese document. Chinese set down in ink on a page was so much darker than Japanese. It gave Hanshichi the creeps, a bit.

" I think maybe you'd be more comfortable somewhere else," said Yasaburo.

Hanshichi had no objection. They went into a tea room.

"I didn't pay as much attention as I should have to what you said last time. That is an admission of incompetence. Anyway, tell me again. How many times did you go the teacher's house after the young teacher died?"

"Three times. I'm sure of that. The last time gave me my excuse not to go again. And there wouldn't have been many times anyway, she was off in such a hurry. The last time was in May. The other times were early in the year and I think maybe in March. They didn't amount to much. She wanted to adopt me, meaning I think that she wanted to marry me, and she was the age of my mother. I have to take over the shop and it wouldn't have been possible."

"There was someone else involved the last time, I think you said?"

"A man was waiting for her when we got back from the bath. It was at the bath that she picked me up."

"And how did he give you your excuse?"

"He was very unpleasant, in a way that made it easy for me to run away. I think he was jealous. It seems ridiculous, but I think he was. I ran off without saying good-bye, and made up my mind not to go again. She never had much chance to ask me, of course."

"Can you describe him?"

"I can see him. But there's not much to describe. He must have been on the near side of middle age, maybe in his forties, and he had a very dark skin."

"A pretty low-class type, you're saying?"

Yasaburo did not say yes and he did not say no. It was true, however, that people tended to be less refined the darker their skins. The darker the skin the lower the class.

"If you can see him so clearly it's silly to ask whether you'd recognize him if you saw him again."

Yasaburo agreed. "You're the guest," he said, paying the bill.

Hanshichi liked this and he liked the young man.

Matsu, meanwhile, was finding old-fashioned methods rather fun.

He went first to discuss matters with the boys over there east of the river. They offered no objection to his investigations and told him a few things.

They were not surprised that Hanshichi had detected a serpentine smell in the district north of Ryogoku and its temple. As Hanshichi had pointed out, peddlers of a kind lodged together. As to whether this meant a conspiracy in restraint of trade the boys had no opinion.

"But aren't snakes a sort of peculiar article to be peddling?"

"They don't peddle snakes. They use them for demonstrations. They sell charms to keep off snakes. You know. The Fish Pond down that way."

The man made a gesture in the direction of Osaka. The "down that way" had to be on the road to Osaka, or Kyoto, although Osaka was generally more interesting for the son of Edo. Since it was assumed he knew of the place Matsu had to pretend that he did. As a matter of fact he did remember having heard of it, more literally the Pond of the Two Carp, signifying two varieties of carp. It had a famous shrine that sold protection against something, and it might as well be snakes. Later he looked it up in a chronicle of a journey to Osaka and found that it did indeed specialize in talismans for the subjugation of reptiles.

"Isn't selling charms to keep off snakes a little dishonest?"

"Yes," replied his informant in an altogether matter-of-fact way.

The police did not consider it their duty to protect the public from fraud. Let the buyer beware. There were foolish buyers all over the place and they were no threat to Lord Tokugawa.

So Matsu went to the house designated by Hanshichi.

He did not choose to operate by stealth. Announcing himself to be in the official service, he asked whether there were other establishments that specialized in snakes. Yes, there were, and all of them were near by. Did they exchange information? Yes, they did. The man did not ask any credentials of Matsu. If the statement about official business proved false why then of course Matsu would have his head chopped off. Matsu half wished that he were not so young that he would have to learn a new way.

He was about to ask whether instances of thievery had recently come to the man's attention when a vaguely familiar face appeared. It was not the man Matsu had paid closest attention to, the one accused of thievery. It could well be the other.

"I was very rude yesterday," said Matsu.

In many languages this could have been a puzzling statement, but in Japanese it often referred to nothing at all.

"Oh by no means. I was rude myself."

This too referred to nothing at all. But the man's countenance was questioning. Clearly he could recall no meeting, nothing which might be the occasion for even a conventional apology.

"I'm from the police. On the boat yesterday afternoon you were having an argument. Somebody took something from you. I was wondering if I might help."

"Thank you. It was just a friendly disagreement."

"You didn't seem very friendly."

Clearly the man wished to drop the subject.

Having nothing against him, Matsu did not resort to old-fashioned methods. He persisted, however, politely.

"Can you tell me something about him?"

"Well, he's a crook. And it's about all I know. You may think I'm lying when I say I don't even know his name. I hardly knew him until it turned out he wanted something of mine."

Not wanting to make an enemy of the man Matsu did not ask what it was. There was an element of fraud involved, and it would not do to put the man on his guard. In any case he thought he knew. Hanshichi thought he knew, and Matsu very rarely disagreed with Hanshichi.

"Do you have any idea where he lives?"

"I doubt that he lives anywhere. He moves around. People like him do. But if you have a few days to spend wandering up and down the street he'll be coming by. He said he'd bring it back. After we had our fight yesterday. I think he was afraid I'd go to you people. I don't know what all he has to hide, but it must be plenty."

The man clearly did not doubt Matsu's credentials. If "it" meant the snake, Matsu might have said it would not be the same one. The original snake was in custody.

"Might he come today?"

"I have no idea. It's possible."

Matsu might not be in a position to spend several days loitering, but he had nothing else to do this afternoon, and no orders from Hanshichi other than to sniff out snakes. Luck was as important in this business of prying and spying as skill and knowledge. He had already had good luck in coming upon the (to him) less interesting of the adversaries on the boat, and he might have more good luck. The day's mission had been as successful thus far as he could have hoped. Besides, there was another person to be on the lookout for in this part of town: the other Saburo, he of the Yokohama matter.

So he walked this way and that, always keeping in sight of the entrance to the snake center. If he had been one of the wealthy parts of town, with their streets following the paths of the farmers and their oxen, he might not have gone more than a few steps in any direction without losing sight of it. These less affluent districts were always burning down, however, and it had come to be that they were rebuilt in rectangles. Sometimes the rectangles did not join one another ideally, but the rectangular principle was there all the same. North of Ryogoku Bridge the problem was not twisting streets. It was that from a certain distance he could not recognize faces. So each time someone entered the snake place he had to hurry back. There were not many such people. Those who went in seemed to be only men (no women) who lodged there.

Another good thing about the poorer parts of town was that they were well provided with small eating and drinking places. He went into one of the latter with a good view of the snake house.

It was, as so many such places were, snug and friendly. He did not learn much about the snake house that had not already known, but this was confirmed. The snakes were used to confirm the efficacy of the talismans which their keepers sold.

"Does it seem to you an honest business?"

"I think they sell mostly to women."

Matsu accepted this as a good answer.

Matsu did not mind waiting. He was a good drinker, and he liked the place. He would not mind becoming something of a regular customer. He had a thought or two if waiting did not work. The boys with whom he had consulted before beginning his inquiry would know something if indeed the man was a professional criminal. This was perhaps the most valuable piece of information he had come upon. And he was in no hurry. There was no pressure to solve a case which everyone thought obvious. Nor did Hanshichi seem inclined to rush him. Today, tomorrow, any day.

But once more he was in luck. He was sure that the man approaching the snake house was his man.

The time had come for a bit of bullying—for old-fashioned methods.

He told the keeper of the place that he would be back and rushed out. No objection was voiced to this somewhat erratic behavior. The man probably suspected what was afoot.

He accosted the man at the door of the snakes.

"We've met before. You may not remember me, but I remember you. It was on the boat across the river yesterday."

The man made as if to leave.

"I'm from the police. What I want of you is this: I want to know where you live, and if you don't live anywhere, maybe you can tell me where I can find you again if I need you, and what time of what day you'll be there. Understand? You have a tongue, I suppose. Or did you or someone bite it off?" He would have had to admit, if challenged, that that would not be easy to do, but he expected no challenge and got none. It was just a manner of speaking.

He had taken the man by the collar of his kimono. The man tried to shake free.

"You aren't talking?" He was not giving the man much chance to talk. He was showing who was boss. "Is your mouth stuffed full of something? Well, spit it out, and spit out what I need to know. You aren't talking? Maybe I should knock out some teeth? I could do that too, and I can't think of much you could do without getting yourself sent off to some island, if you last long enough. And I could do other things. Look at all the mosquitoes. It's early for them. Maybe they know they have a feast in store. That nice man over there will lend us some vinegar I'm sure."

"All right, all right. Give me a chance. If that's not asking too much."

Matsu was wondering whether this sort of thing would work in Yokohama, and doubting it. Yes, there was something to be said for giving an officer of the law a free hand.

The man did not give an address. A genuine address was a rarity in Edo. Sections of the city had names but streets did not. Within a section no one paid much attention to numbers even when, and this was rare, they in theory existed.

"Turn right on the third cross street beyond the bridge and look for a Chinese drug store full of snakes and lizards and it's the second house up the way. And what is it you want to see me about?"

Matsu did not answer. He had never heard of habeas-corpus, and it had no place in Lord Tokugawa's way of doing things.

"Write down everything you've just said. People are more

likely to tell the truth when it's in writing. I always carry brush and ink with me. Clever of me, don't you think?"

Matsu did always have in his stomacher, the place for carrying things, a rather dashing little secretarial set. It could be useful, and he liked bringing it out, and showing that he was a young man of some style. The case was lacquer, and good. Before long it could find a confident niche in a curio shop. Not just everyone had a taste for such things, though their frequency was higher in Edo than in most places, higher, perhaps, indeed, than anywhere else in the land. And if in the land, why then also in the world.

"One thing more. What's your friend's name?"

"I don't have any friends that you would know."

"You know who I mean. The man on the boat."

This man obliged with a name, which seemed likely enough. There was no family name.

He went to the little drinking place and paid his bill. He would have done so anyway, but it was possible that he would need it again. Then he headed for Kanda to report to Hanshichi. He was sure to be praised. Hanshichi was never reluctant to praise good work.

"You've just about broken the case," said Hanshichi. "Do you want to see it through to the end, or do you want me to take over?"

It was a moment for modesty. "I'd learn a lot from seeing how you manage it. And the one we need now is the young fellow from the hanging shop, and he's your young fellow. We should be quick about it. He knows he's being chased. I doubt that he's lying. We could run him up for that even if all the rest turns out to be false leads. But the truth today isn't necessarily the truth tomorrow."

"I couldn't put it better myself. Let's go find Yasaburo."

They found him hard at work, and begged leave to take him away from it for a little while. This was not an hour at which the man had said he would be at home, but, as Matsu had suggested, home might have changed by the time the hour came.

Yasubaro was amenable. He had been about to call it a day.

The man's directions seemed accurate. They turned up the designated street just west of the river and found the shop full of snakes and lizards and other Chinese delectables. Next door to it was a neat little house like many others up and down the street. It seemed too modest to be a criminal's house, but then they had no reason to think that the man was a professional criminal. Deeds of violence often stood in isolation, sad deviations from an ordinary life. Matsu almost felt sorry for the man. More hardened, Hanshichi did not. Unobtrusive citizens could do horrible things.

They had come none too soon. Preparations for a move were in progress.

"That's the one," said Yasaburo of the man who was supervising them.

Hanshichi did not bother with introductions.

"Out with it. What were the two of you? I mean you and the dance teacher on the Shogun's Road. Were you lovers? Were you married? Whatever you were you hadn't seen her for a while. You came in and found her with a young man she had picked up somewhere. She didn't seem glad to see you. So neither of you was happy and you had a fight after the fellow left. So you decided you'd get rid of her. You'd put on a show. You stole a snake from the man across the river, the man who uses snakes in his business. You're pretty good at staging things. So you strangled her and put the snake around her neck, and made the world think that her daughter had put a curse on her or come and strangled her, the way ghosts will, you know, especially women's ghosts. Like something out of the variety halls. But, if you think you can get by with it, you think you can go out in the middle of a dark night without a lantern. You're a cool one. A little snake. But you're caught, and you can't expect anyone to help you. Come on, now. Out with it. Is your mouth full? Open it up wide, now, and give us the truth. You won't? I don't want to beat you up, but I may have to."

Edo speech, especially male speech, was always rapid-fire, but this was a virtuoso performance. The man allowed himself to be led to the offices by the river. He maintained his silence, but that he was guilty seemed obvious. The police of Edo may not have had careful rules of evidence, but they had a sense for things. One day in autumn, at execution grounds to north of the city, the man was beheaded.

"What put you onto the business of the snakes?" asked Matsu, as they were on their way back from the offices by the river. "Everyone else (me too) took it for granted that the daughter did her in."

"Not everyone who knew the daughter," said Yasaburo.

"I still have the snake. I'll show you."

Back at his place, Hanshichi took out the snake. Then he took out a card and held it over the snake's head. The snake bowed.

"See? There you have the element of fakery. The fellow that had his snake stolen isn't such a nice fellow either, but I don't consider that any of our business. The snake was trained to bow when someone holds a card over it. That's the evidence, if you're gullible enough, that the charms have an effect on snakes."

"It would have been a perfect day if I'd run into Saburo."

"Don't start thinking it's all luck."

"Thank you."

The two young ones both said it, for different reasons.

A few days later Matsu went down to Yokohama, to check on things. And maybe, thought Hanshichi, to enjoy himself, and who could reprove him for it? He came back with information which they thought could be taken to close their Yokohama case. They could conceivably do more, but why bother? They agreed about the answer to this last question.

"One of the things I found out finishes the case in one way. The magistrate's office has found out that Thompson's, you know, the English company Lloyd worked for, is missing a tailor's dummy. If there ever was much of a puzzle over the foreign head there isn't any more."

"You don't mean that the English consulate helped them? That is a surprise."

"But of course you can't really believe they did. The consul said it was none of his business. Sort of funny when you think about it. After all it was an English company that lost the thing, and the consulate had no intention of doing anything about it. That's the way they are."

"I'm not sure it's a good idea to think they're all alike."

"I doubt that it much matters what I think, and the people at the magistrate's office don't think that at all. Maybe they overdo the differences."

"What harm can that do?"

"A very smart fellow up there in the magistrate's office said the Americans are the only ones we might be able to use against anyone else. The others will stick together. So whatever differences there might be don't matter. Said this smart fellow up in the magistrate's office. Anyhow, I meant the English. Everyone thinks he's better than everyone else and they hardly speak to each other. And they're so far from home."

"And the other thing?"

"It's a little sad, but I don't think I'll shed many tears over it. Lloyd has killed himself."

"Oh. Why?" Hanshichi did not seem exactly devastated either.

"I doubt that anyone really knows. What is clear is that Thompson had had enough of him and was sending him back to England. They told him he was lucky they'd pay his way. And why didn't he want to go? He didn't say. Or anyhow the boys in the magistrate's office say he didn't. But, don't you agree, sex is about the only think strong enough to make a man kill himself rather than go away. Don't underestimate the powers of Japanese women."

"I wouldn't dream of it. Anyway: case finished. It might not be a bad thing."

Matsu thought he knew why, but waited to be told.

"We won't lose any face. We can shout to the world that we were frustrated by the "unequal treaties."

Hanshichi did not think much about politics, but he hated the "unequal treaties."

They set out to pass this new intelligence on to the constable by the river

"I'm a little sorry for one reason. I wish I had found Saburo."

"Why? To lead you from one whorehouse to another?"

"A friend who knows something about Yokohama could be useful."

"In the years we have ahead of us. I'm glad I have fewer of them than you."

"Well speaking of the devil." It happened that Japanese and English contained very similar expressions. "Hello."

"Now we can really consider the case closed."

## About the Author

Translations by Edward Seidensticker, Professor Emeritus of Japanese at New York's Columbia University, have introduced two generations of English native-speakers to the masterpieces of classical and modern Japanese literature—Junichiro Tanizaki's *The Makioka Sisters*, Nobel Prize winner Yasunari Kawabata's *Snow Country*, Yukio Mishima's *The Decay of the Angel*), and the works of Nagai Kafu.

He is arguably most renowned as a translator for rendering in its entirety Murasaki Shikibu's *The Tale of Genji* (Knopf, 1976), generally considered to be the first modern novel of world literature.

In addition, the author's first book on Tokyo, *Low City, High City: Tokyo from Edo to the Earthquake*, looks at the time period between the Meiji Restoration in 1868 and the great earthquake in 1923. *Tokyo Rising: The City Since the Great Earthquake* published in 1990, covers the time period after the great Kanto earthquake of September 1, 1923.